I0760648

PASS ME A LIFE

Kennedy Bennett Fox

Pass Me a Life

www.kennedybennettfox.com

ISBN: 978-1-923289-92-5 (Paperback)

A catalogue record for this book is available from the National Library of Australia

Cover Design: Kennedy Bennett Fox and Clark & Mackay
Format and Typeset: Kennedy Bennett Fox and Clark & Mackay
Published by Kennedy Bennett Fox and Clark & Mackay

Proudly printed in Australia by Clark & Mackay

You don't love someone for their looks,
or their clothes, or their fancy car, but because
they sing a song only you can hear.
—Oscar Wilde

DEDICATION

I dedicate my first book to my parents,
Stella and Gordon,
who always taught me to be myself.

AUTHOR'S NOTE

This account shares a story about a gay relationship.

It is intended to provide insight into how love does not care about gender, race, religion, or any other obstacle or boundary.

I hope that readers will come away firstly thinking what a beautiful love story and then, with an understanding of how challenging a gay relationship can still be in a world that claims to be caring and open.

Note: Footy First and Millurat are a fictional organisation and place, as are all the characters in this novel.

PROLOGUE

We lay there sipping our morning cuppa, as we had done for many years. John smiled at me, kissed me with, "On good days, I love to remember those good times. Sometimes when those bad days float in, I try and go back to good days. We had lots of good ones, didn't we?"

"Yes, we did, young man, but everyone has bad days, and some of ours were really tough. But all that is in the past now; just good memories now, John."

"You should write your story, Robbie."

"It is our story, John, very much ours. We shared everything."

"Yes, we did. Write our story please, I can help you remember," and he smiled at me, that smile that captured my heart those many years ago and has never dimmed.

CHAPTER 1

I stood looking at the row of shirts: *What to wear*?

My sister Ruth had insisted I go to my nephew's twentieth birthday party. "You know, he tells everyone you are his favourite uncle."

"We have no other siblings, and you married an only child ... stiff competition!"

"Well, he does admire you," continued Ruth. "Anyway, there will be some single men there; we might get you settled yet with someone decent."

My sister always reminded me that my two previous relationships were big mistakes, which I was forced to agree with. Relationship mistakes are hard enough to bear in reality, but compounded when everyone in the entire universe agrees they were a disaster, and asks, "Why did you do it?"

I always moved on by saying, "Good sex." Besides, Ruth reminded me, I was having a big birthday the same day.

"We can toast you both."

Why do people single out big birthdays? They are all big. You just got through another year.

I always knew, when my nephew was born on my birthday, it was not a blessing. Sometimes, you want to escape them. Children having birthdays are a big event, so when I was thirty-three, and he had a jumping castle for the children ... poor old Uncle Robbie was expected to join in the fun.

I smile to myself about that birthday. Was it revenge when, after being forced to eat a slice of revolting mock cream birthday cake, the colour of which was never designed to see the light of day, I was dragged off to experience the joys of the jumping castle? After a few minutes of tortuous jumping to the squeals of delight of the onlookers, and without warning, I threw up all over twins in matching outfits. Ruth was not amused, but I did escape the parties for the next three years.

Arriving at Ruth and Barry's place awash with balloons (fortunately, no jumping castle), Ruth hugged me and Barry shook my hand at a distance. Ruth always said he was totally at ease with me being gay, so like him, I always gave an extended handshake. My nephew Jimmy came over, hugged me, and we exchanged a mutual birthday greeting.

An older couple came over and were introduced as Tony and Merryl Willadoro; they were neighbours who had moved in next door some time ago. Jimmy became friends with their sons.

A voice behind me said, "Hi everyone, I'm Johnno, been doing some footy practice with Jimmy here."

Turning, I came face to face with a young man whose smile should never have been let loose on the world. He put his hand out. Tall, athletic, with dark hair that fell about his face in waves, skin like tanned 'Gladwrap', he appeared to be relaxed in a controlled manner. He was ninety-eight percent Adonis, yet that smile ...

Hey, being a novelist, I like to expand on the detail!

Anyway, we exchanged pleasantries and apart from being flashed 'that smile', I was ignored, which was the story of my life. From the conversation, I gathered he was the younger Willadoro son.

"Where's Susan?" Johnno's dad queried.

Looking a bit uneasy, he replied, "Haven't seen her for ages. I didn't ask her; she wouldn't know anyone."

Scoffing, his dad said, "She dumped you like all the rest?"

He coloured. I excused myself and headed to the bar. It presented as a long afternoon. Johnno was obviously your good-looking young macho man with women frequently falling at his feet. In typical style, he was always moving on to another. Obviously, his father could observe. *Well, I guess he will 'work the room'*, I thought to myself.

Asking for a glass of bubbles at the bar, a voice behind me spoke, "I'll have one too."

It was the not-ever-to-be-let-loose smiler.

"Bubbles, young man? Is that what young macho men drink these days?"

"Is that how you see me? Perceptions can be deceptive, but I'll still stick to bubbles. So, Uncle Robbie, if I may call you that? Happy birthday."

I explored the expression on his face. *Was he playing with me*? However, that smile always got in the way.

"Thanks. My sister has obviously been working overtime."

"Sorry about my dad. He's obsessed about me getting married, or even just having a girlfriend."

"Know the feeling, same when I was young."

"Parents, and particularly my dad, is determined to see me married; irritates me no end. I think I am too young to be worried about it yet."

Even I thought that was a 'hallo' (pronounced *hell-oh*) answer. I enquired how old he was.

"Twenty-seven. And you, if that's not too rude?"

"Well, young man, fifty today."

Still smiling—smile torture, I'd call it—he commented, "In good nick."

He made a comment that my nephew was a nice guy. "Must run in the family." Awkward pause, then looking straight at me, "Is your wife, or partner here, or are you single?"

"What? You get to the point quickly, young man."

"Sorry, get nervous in company, blurt things out. Don't mean to be rude, sorry."

He continued, "Okay, change of subject, social chat, can I ask what work you do? Are you a mechanic, in case my car needs repairs? Or accountant, always handy; a doctor?"

"Wrong on all counts, young man, I write some novels—still trying to crack the big one—articles for magazines, things like that."

He frowned. "Gossip kinda stuff, is it?"

"No such crap. Respectable writers avoid that. So, what do you do, young man?"

"Play footy."

"Yes, you said that, but what's your real job?" He looked at me and grinned. "You're quite a character."

My nephew sidled up and announced he was taking Johnno to tour the room. As they left without any sense of reason, I called out and am not sure why, "By the way, John, the answer to your question is yes, I'm single."

He turned, looked me in the eye with, "No one ever calls me John."

"Sorry," I blurted out.

"No, I like it. You get exclusive rights to that." He turned and left.

My sister appeared chuckling. "Well, big brother, you are the envy of the room."

"What do you mean?"

"Well," she replied with a smile, but not—although I love my sister dearly—as good as the 'smile boy'. "The famous

Johnno Willadoro is not noted for long chats. He's a very private man, they say."

"He seemed a nice guy, if not a bit forward."

"What do you mean 'forward'?"

"He wanted to know if I was married or single. Thought it was odd, as I had only just met him. Still, young people can be like that, you know, in your face."

"What did you say?"

"Indicated he was a bit forward but as he left, said yes. Have no idea why I said that to him. Anyway, what do you mean, famous?"

"Oh," said Ruth, "I forgot you don't follow football. He plays for Australia, their top player. Everyone adores him, obviously, except you."

"Oh God! He said he played footy, and I asked him what his real job was!"

"You did what?" barked Ruth.

"Well, he did seem amused by it."

"Well, don't look now, but he is staring directly at you."

"I'll leave, must think I'm an idiot."

"Stay!" demanded Ruth.

Johnno glanced over at Jimmy's uncle. Hair turning to silver, stocky body, though not overweight, smartly dressed, relaxed, and easy to talk to. That was strange for him. He liked what he saw, but why? *What's making me interested? Geez, he's an old guy for heaven's sake and shit, he's a guy!* Johnno's mind raced.

What was the force that was working within him? He found, even in that brief time together, he was comfortable just being with the older guy. He felt relaxed, which was something new for him. He didn't understand it, but sensed deep down he had no power to stop it. He needed, no, he wanted to explore it further.

Johnno slowly worked the room. He was an old hand at it now, but this time he moved quickly, suddenly appearing behind Robbie, without warning.

"Do you ever knock, young man?"

Mr Smile replied, "You and your sister look close."

"Yes, we are. Just told me I was an idiot."

"Really? Why was that?"

"She told me what your real job was."

He laughed. "Loved it! First time it has ever happened; means we have started off on a level playing field."

"A level playing field. What do you mean? Hope you don't want me to play."

"God no, get sick of constant footy chat. Love playing but want to leave it on the field. Don't you like to take a break from your work now and then?"

"Yes, clears the head."

"So, what does single Uncle Robbie like to do at home alone?"

I felt his eyes piercing me, keen to explore.

"You are an inquisitive young man, very upfront for someone who is supposed to be shy."

"I rarely find someone I feel at ease talking to. In fact, I rarely talk much at all, but find I am only around you once and I can't shut myself up, which is so unusual for me."

"Thought you would be surrounded by people?"

"Sure, always am, but you can still be lonely in a group of people. Jimmy told me you made the uncooked veggie rolls. Tasty, so you enjoy cooking?"

"Yes, I do. They are a Vietnamese recipe, meant to be uncooked."

"Really, unusual, so you like cooking and obviously travel. Where do you go?"

"Asia, Europe over the years. What about you?"

"Only London a few times to play footy but didn't see much. Was so excited to be in London and really wanted to see everything. The guys just wanted to pub crawl, hit the discos, and find a root. Suggested seeing the sights and they all laughed at me; called me a 'wanker'. Told my dad on the phone and he blasted me saying, "Don't suggest such things, they'll all think you're a pansy." That upset me.

"That your dad thought you were gay, or you had a thirst for knowledge away from the field?"

"Neither, I know some gay guys, no issue for me. But why stereotype people? So, you enjoyed your trips?"

"Very much. You need to travel more. It broadens your horizons. Just like reading. Do you read much? "

"At school a few books, but not much since, training, social things I need to do take up my time, so no reading. Maybe you could suggest some books for me."

"What sort of books interest you?"

Laughing, Johnno answered, "Ones that are a bit edgy."

"Edgy?"

He winked. "Books that push relationship boundaries."

"Hmmm, you are turning out to be an interesting young man. Put your mobile number into my phone so I can text you suggested titles from some I have at home."

"Maybe I can call around and borrow them?"

I looked at him, wondering where this was leading.

"Sorry, I can just buy them."

"No John, happy to lend them to you, okay?

John's dad came up to him, ignoring me. "Johnno, come and meet some young people here who are fans." He took his arm and pulled him away. John looked back at me. His face was blank.

Topping up on bubbles, before it ran out, I moved back inside and onto the front veranda to relax alone. Ruth would not be happy if I left early.

I then enjoyed some quiet time. My mind reflected on the man called John. He was an intriguing character. I knew he held a story, so how would it unfold? The first thought an old guy thinks of is 'sugar daddy'. John, however, would, even at his age, have more money than me; he could attract any girl, or even guys. *Maybe there's a novel in it*? I had an inward chuckle.

Sometime later, my thoughts and peace were broken by a fresh glass of bubbles presented to me with a query if he could join me. I nodded yes. I was curious about this man whom I had just met and yet he continued to seek me out.

Sitting beside me, he commented. "My dad can be unsociable at times."

Grinning at him, I responded, "You are a kind son, John."

His eyes lit up as he replied, "Do you feel like going somewhere for a coffee and having a chat, Robbie? I'd really like to talk to you some more. I feel I need to explore this. I am enjoying it; it's new for me."

"Ruth has coffee here."

"Sure, but it comes with an army of footy fans."

"People may ask why we are leaving together to have a coffee, when there is coffee here."

He laughingly said with a wink. "Sure, but if you leave through the front door, I can climb out through the toilet window."

"You are joking, John. Why?"

"Let's find out, shall we, and remember, John is yours, and yours only."

CHAPTER 2

Ruth rang early the next morning. "Are you alone?"

"Of course, always am."

"Well," she proceeded, "after you said your goodbyes, no one could find Johnno. He told Jimmy he was slipping away for a meeting and not to make a big announcement, as it would take ages to say goodbyes. After seeing you both chatting away together, I thought you might have struck gold."

"Ruth, he's straight, has girlfriends; anyway, you know I don't do young."

"Well," she added, "he is twenty-seven, not that far from fifty, and a good catch."

"I'm not a fisherman, either. Ruth, did you hear me? He's straight."

"Old grumpy bear this morning," she commented. "Maybe ... umm ... no sleep last night?"

"Forget this nonsense. He was not here at any time. After I left, yes, we did meet for coffee. He said he only wanted to talk. He really wanted a sounding board because he has no one he feels he can safely talk to. Incredibly sad, in what he had to say. He came across to me as a lonely guy. A famous adored footballer, worshiped by everyone, put on a pedestal, just trying to find someone he can trust to talk to.

"I really felt for him. His dad and Footy First have mapped out his life. And all this is just between us please,

Ruth. He poured his heart out. He feels lost, the way his life is panning out. His outpourings gave me a sense he could trust me, so don't get any of your ideas. This is total trust I share with you. I really hope I helped him."

Ruth sighed and agreed I was a good sounding board. It was an unromantic thought but earned me brownie points.

Curled up in bed, I reflected on my coffee catch up with John. I had wondered why we picked up coffee at a drive-through and drove to the far end of the local park.

He had looked at me and explained, "I can relax here, away from the fans. You have no idea how I feel so much in the spotlight. It never ends."

It made me acutely aware of how his life is shadowed by his fame. This young man did not have the freedom that the rest of us enjoy and take for granted. Sure, it gave him financial stability, but it came at a price. I was unprepared for how much he opened up.

I stopped him and said it would go no further. But it bothered me. *Why me*?

John told me he would not have suggested any personal discussions unless he felt safe with me. He looked me straight in the eye, told me he felt secure with me, an emotion he had not experienced ever before, and he wanted to run with it.

"Robbie, for the first time in my life, I felt safe with someone."

He told me that at the party he mentioned to Jimmy what a nice guy I was. Jimmy had replied that his uncle and his mum were so close he would trust both with his life. Jimmy explained that a few times growing up, his parents wouldn't let him do things he wanted to, but Uncle Robbie was supportive and went in to bat for him. His uncle talked through the issues with his parents and even though his uncle had no children, they understood the basis of his arguments. In the end, his folks agreed. Jimmy said he was like a second dad, although he loved his parents very much.

John's training as a footballer started early. As his dad discovered soon on, that John's older brothers had no talent for it, so he was the designated hero to be. His dad ran a successful building company, so Tony Junior and Ginge joined the company as soon as they left school. No choice. Their dad told them when Johnno retired from football, Johnno would take over from him.

John felt so sorry for his brothers, who worked so hard in the business and were particularly good at it. Any time it was raised, John told his dad and brothers he had no interest in it. John told them the boys would run it well. His dad always scoffed at that.

Life revolved around training completely. When he expressed an interest in cooking in the kitchen with his mum, it was quickly squashed by his dad. "Women's work," was his father's comment. "Your brothers are fit for that."

John's career progressed, and he found he had a talent for the game. He really enjoyed it, but unlike his teammates, he wanted a life away from the field. A string of ladies always lined up for him at functions, and of course, the girls loved being seen on the arm of a star footballer, but they wanted more at the end of the night.

He held my gaze, saying he had never told anyone before that he did not enjoy all the attention the women gave him. He had issues he did not understand, and a few of the girls talked. They said he was a 'dud fuck'. He blushed. I could see his eyes well up. He did not understand these feelings he was experiencing; he felt there was no one he could talk to about this confusion. Being so well known, he trusted no one, and knew his dad would not understand.

He opened up his feelings to me and wondered if I could understand how wonderful it was to find someone he could truly trust. "Robbie, I trust you, please, please don't let me down."

And I knew I never could.

I felt so much for this young man; on the surface, he appeared so confident, but inside, he was struggling. Gently, I queried if I could ask him a personal question.

"Fire away," came the response.

Carefully, I suggested he might be having a struggle with his sexuality, hoping I wouldn't get punched out. He stared at me, tears running down his face, nodding yes.

"Take your time John."

Eventually, he told me he was trying to understand what was happening; it was all new to him, with no one to talk to. When he met me, he felt something which he didn't understand either; it was all so strange. Talking to me seemed easy, like he had known me for ages, but even that he didn't understand.

"You were a person I had only just met, and older. Maybe that's why I felt comfortable. I needed to take a chance. I had reached a point where I desperately needed to talk to someone."

He took my hand and just held it for ages.

"Robbie, it feels warm. Sorry, you must think I'm crazy." He studied me, anguish in his eyes, tears streaming. "I just dream of being held tightly by someone who genuinely wants me. Stupid, I know."

"No John, everyone has a right to that." Then I slowly put my arms around him as he sobbed.

Because of his position, the media were on to everything he did, so he had been scared to try and experiment. He had to find someone he could trust. He told me he was shit scared.

When overseas on tour, he had tried several gay bars and saunas but found no joy, just men who wanted sex and no talk, just wanting his body. John admitted he was excited about seeing naked guys but felt empty after his encounters with the men. I felt so sad for him. Adored by everyone but lacking love.

The phone ringing jolted me out of my reflections. "Hi, it's Johnno. Sorry to ring so late, but I have been plucking up the courage to ring and thank you for coffee and listening to me. Felt I probably bored you. But it really helped me. It gave me a lot to think about, thanks."

"Not at all John, I enjoyed our chat, was happy to talk. Always ready to. Appreciate you need a shoulder."

"Great, I wanted to take you to lunch, sort of thank you."

"You don't have to do that."

"I know, but kinda wanted to see you again."

Silence.

"Are you there Robbie?"

"Yes, John, here."

"If you don't want to, all good."

"It is a bit sudden, maybe in a week or so, okay?"

"Sure, thanks for listening." He hung up. I felt possibly I didn't handle that well. *No, just reading too much into it.*

Later that week, my nephew Jimmy rang, which he doesn't often do.

"Hi Jimmy, what's up?"

"Well, funny question to ask you, but have you seen Johnno since the party?"

I moved to cautious mode. "Why, what's up?

"Well, since the party, he's been acting weird. I asked him to kick the footy around and he says he hasn't got the time. Ginge says he is always snappy at home, missed a training session with no word or excuse. I mentioned it to

Mum, and she said ask your uncle, so not sure what she meant by that? What do you think she meant by that? He disappeared from the party out of the blue about the time you left. Odd."

"Jimmy, maybe he is just having a bad time. His dad is always on his back."

"How did you know that?"

"He made reference to it at the party, and I saw how his dad had a go at him as soon as he arrived."

"Yes, I agree. Just thought I would ask. He is a great bloke. Still don't know why Mum thought you would know."

I sat in silence after the phone call ended.

Should I do anything? Had I given any indication to John that I was leading him on? *That's crazy, we just talked*. Couldn't see that I showed any feelings towards him, and why would he be interested in me, anyway? I struggled to understand, but even more, I knew he was struggling. *Why me*?

I picked up the phone.

Half an hour later, he arrived.

"Hi Robbie."

"Hi John, come in. What's going on?"

"So pleased you rang. I thought you didn't like me."

"What gave you that idea? I just needed some space. I didn't know what was happening, why you wanted to keep talking with me. I was confused about what was going on and wasn't sure where you were coming from."

"Sorry Robbie, I was just so excited to find someone I felt comfortable with, someone I could trust, and talk freely to. Never felt like this with anyone. My mind was spinning. You are so self-assured. I felt really safe with you, trusting you."

"Even I can be insecure."

He half smiled and seemed to bite his lip as he added, in rather a shy tone, "So, we're still on that level playing field?"

"Yes, we are. Okay, how about a spot of dinner, then I will pack you off home after we have arranged a lunch date, okay?"

He smiled. "Yes, I can live with that."

CHAPTER 3

Another early morning 'Ruth call' and I answered with, "Good morning, my darling sister."

"Cut the crap, big brother, it's straight-talking time."

"What are you talking about?"

"Here's the scenario. Johnno has not been himself all week—moody, not eating, missed two training sessions without notice. Take note, he has never done this before! Where was I? Oh yes, snapped if asked a question, pissed Jimmy off when he suggested a catch up to toss the ball. Then Jimmy rings nice Uncle Robbie—"

"At the suggestion of a little bird that was told to keep her beak shut," I interrupted.

"Be that as it may, Uncle Robbie knows nothing of course, but after that call, surprise, surprise, Johnno gets a call, rushes out of the house and comes home later about 9 pm, all smiles and happy as ever. Are you the fucking fairy godmother who waved the magic wand?"

Silence.

"Or dare I add, waved something else?"

"Don't be vulgar."

"Fess up, darling brother. What's going on?"

"Okay but promise to keep your bird beak glued this time."

"Robbie, you know I love a secret."

"I may have rung John

Ruth interjected, "Excuse me, why is it always John and not Johnno?"

"It's a code, Ruth, men's business."

"God help us, are you two part of a secret society?"

"I may have rung him and suggested a chat. I gave him dinner—I heard he had not been eating."

"Anything else, may I add?"

"A light beer and sent him home."

"I still think you have done something."

"You always said my chicken yellow curry was to die for."

"I will accept that explanation for the moment, so keep on your toes. No one wants him like that again, hear me?"

"So, you think I can control him? And what's it to you, anyway?"

"I'm just saying that since he met you, his behaviour has been erratic, to say the least, with highs and lows. So, I'm not inferring anything, but if my darling brother is causing the highs, I would not be at all upset. Got it?"

"Yes, ma'am. Goodbye."

CHAPTER 4

I walked into the Shingle Inn at the Brisbane Town Hall and wondered why John had chosen it. A bit old-fashioned for a young man who the world adores. But looking at the booths and the old ladies there, I guessed it would give him the privacy he needed. He waved to me, and I walked over and sat opposite him.

"Hi Robbie, sorry for the lunch place, but we can be alone here. You may have guessed by now that my movements spark interest and I wanted lunch to be just us, so we could talk freely in private."

"John, I do understand and it's not an issue for me. You need a shoulder, and I am happy to be there to talk with you. Anything I can do to help is fine by me."

"Thanks Robbie, but I need to be upfront with you. Since I met you, my mind has been racing as I see you as more than someone just to talk to. My world has gone crazy since we met, and I am trying to come to terms with understanding what's it all about. I never thought I would be able to say it, but I know now that I want to be with a man. There, I have said it ... wow! You triggered that.

"If you feel threatened by that, I will understand if you get up and leave now, but (smiling, oh god that smile) the omelettes here are yummy."

"Wow, John, I need to process all that. What do sporty people say ... 'came out of left field'? We really do need to talk, however, not sure where to start?"

"Robbie, just order, then we'll talk on a full stomach. That always works for me." Then that smile. I felt weak. "You are a charmer, Mr Willadoro, I'll give you that. My world has gone confusion plus since I met you, so I guess I'd better stay for the omelette."

"That's great to hear, Robbie. Choose as many fillings in the omelette as you like."

"John, I can see why you rose to the top; you know how to win." Still that smile.

"Good, settled. I talked a lot at our coffee date about me, so now it's your turn. I want to know all about you. Tell me all; what you like doing when you are not writing. Love affairs. What you look for in a man; why you enjoy writing and anything else you think I need to know."

"Wow, young man, for someone who told me that he was trying to understand the feelings he was experiencing, you get to the point, don't you?!"

"I hope talking about you will help me understand more of why I am attracted to you. You are constantly in my mind, yes, always. Wow, said that too now."

"I don't think 'wow' sums it up, young man. Need a stiff drink after this. Well, I guess they only do coffee here. So will just have to throw heaps of chilli sauce on the omelette. That'll spark me up. Okay, here goes ... I've had two relationships, or perhaps a better word is friendships, never got to live with them. Fortunately, they fell apart before that was considered.

"I was much younger, and I guess wanting to experience the joys of the intimacy of being with a man."

"Were they good sex?"

"Is your middle name upfront? I've certainly learnt that about you so far."

"Robbie, I don't understand it. Around you I open up: I don't seem to be able to shut up. I was never like this before meeting you and I love it, like really being alive. Am I a new person? Why? Sorry back to the chat Robbie, keep going please."

"Yes, I guess they were good sex, but I didn't have much before to compare it with. After a while I realised it was just sex, mechanical really, and there wasn't anything else with it."

"Anything else like what?"

"Like affection, desire, passion, and love; all that has escaped me so far. I guess I just wanted some romance in my life."

"I hope I can change all that for you."

"John, you cannot learn everything about a person over one lunch."

"I know that Robbie, so we need to have more, also dinners. You can take me to the theatre, even days at the beach. Hey, I want you to come to one of my football matches. What do you think? Would you cope?"

"Try me."

CHAPTER 5

John had arranged a ticket for me to watch him play. Apart from watching my nephew Jimmy in a few games at school, I was not an avid football fan.

Upon arriving, I presented my ticket to be scanned, which caused a stir. *Great, rejected! I can go home.*

"No," the young lady said. "Mr Burke, you are Mr Willadoro's guest. Samantha will take you to your seat."

I followed her in her skimpy outfit, observing thankfully there were no mossies about that would tuck into so much exposed flesh. I was seated in the front row of what appeared to be a private box. Glad I frocked up. Obviously, the same people always got to sit in this special box because, as a ring-in, I aroused curiosity. Hadn't four million footy fans heard of, or read, the famous ... oh well, okay, well-known novelist, Robert Burke? I doubt it here.

The teams ran on, and we stood for the national anthem. John looked up to my seat, smiled, and did a high five. No one seemed to notice. The game commenced and despite not really knowing what was happening, I observed John was good. I did a lot of jumping up and down and shouting out, "Yeah," hopefully at the right time.

At the end of the match, I wandered into the bar area at the back of the box and got a beer; bubbles were probably not the go. Handing over my credit card, the young lady waved it away. "You are Mr Willadoro's guest."

I was standing alone as John rushed in, receiving a spontaneous cheer. He came up to me and stood there smiling, just looking at me. I could feel every eye in the room upon us. "Great game you played, John, very exciting."

He beamed like an excited boy. Everyone crowded around. They looked at him, then at me. Dare I say there was a feeling of expectancy that hung in the air?

Silence embraced the room.

Wanting to break the ice, I blurted out, "Johnno, great game," and looking around added, "Johnno invited me to the game—my sister lives near his family. Thanks, great game, Johnno."

He glared at me. "Well, better drive you home to your sister." He turned and walked out. I followed.

Outside, he exploded. "What the fuck did you say that shit for?"

"John, they were all looking at both of us, so I thought I could help defuse it."

"I don't need you to do that; I can take care of myself. Get in the car."

This is the first time I had seen him in a mood like this and once in the car, his head fell into the steering wheel.

"I could stand on the roof of this fucking expensive car they made me buy and shout at the world. Let me choose my friends."

"John, don't you like the car?"

"Don't change the fucking subject," he snapped.

He fired the engine, and we roared out of the car park, continuing to drive fast in silence.

A total hush continued as we drove. Then suddenly, he reached out to the car touch screen on the dashboard, and it came to life with a song I recognised: *The First Time.*

The music and lyrics engulfed us.

I turned and looked at John. No expression on his face; he was just looking straight ahead with no emotion. The lyrics ate into my heart. This man was grieving.

I saw moisture in his eyes. I wanted to reach out to him, hoping the warmth of my hand would calm him. I waited, watching, just frozen with him.

He silenced the music as we arrived at my place. He turned to me, immersed in sadness. "Sorry for the outburst. You don't deserve it. I need a drink and a shower."

"Okay, come in." I Pressed the remote, and we drove into my garage. A bright yellow Maserati would be a beacon in my suburb. I wondered if he noticed the small fifteen-year-old sedan he parked beside. Looking at me, he quirked a lip. "Wanna swap cars?"

Laughing, "I cannot see myself in yours."

"Oh, I don't know, all the young spunks would be chasing you. I'd have to work harder." Our eyes met, frozen for seconds, before leaving the yellow beast.

Inside, I gave him a drink. We sat in silence. He raised his glass, and we clinked.

"John, you know I don't follow football, but I could tell you were so good." Just silence. "I don't always get things right."

"Yeah Robbie, you do. Sorry how I reacted, wrong of me. Driving home, I realised you showed me this afternoon what I always thought about you. You are on my side. It was just ... I don't want to make excuses for the people I choose to be with, especially you. You must know by now I like you a lot. Please don't let me fuck this up, please. You are a good man. Hope you'll let me stick around."

"John, your friendship towards me has challenged me, turned my secure world upside down. If you had told me weeks ago, I would have laughed. Do you think a twenty-seven-year-old 'fabbo' footballer and a fifty-year-old boring novelist could work something out?"

I looked at him, and he gazed back at me. Our eyes met yet again, and he added, "Yes, I do. If you don't play football, and I don't write a novel, be a cert, what you say?"

I was smiling at him, with a boring novelist smile thrown in, "Okay, let's see how it all goes. Is that a deal?"

"Deal. I can live with that. Now I need a shower, please. Didn't have one at the club, wanted to get upstairs and see you."

"Follow me." As we walked into my bedroom and I indicated the bathroom, he said, "Wow, upgraded to the ensuite."

"Put that grin away, young man."

He walked in and started to undress. I turned to leave.

"Robbie, stay. I may need you to scrub my back," with a wink.

I froze, wondering where this was going. I had not anticipated a situation like this in these early stages of knowing him. It was moving all so fast. *Help! I am out of my comfort zone.*

"Robbie, look at me. I am still the same guy from the party."

True, but he was not naked then! Years of training had produced—how to I describe it—to hell with it, let go ... a sculptured body that arouses me to ... *no, no, no! Gotta stop there.*

He looked at me, "Come on in, I won't bite."

God, if that was all I had to worry about!

John turned, adjusting the taps. I stood there, unsure of what to do next. Things were moving all too fast.

"Robbie, come on, the hot water will run out."

Looking at him, naked and aroused, it excited me. Yet hell, it scared me. Reluctantly ... yes, please ... believe me ... I gave in, I must admit, with a sense of expectancy, knowing there was now no turning back. So, I climbed in with my back to him, nervous. I guess he wasn't expecting an Adonis. He turned, and I heard his heavy breathing as he whispered in my ear.

"Looks like I may have to wash your back first."

I felt his hands on my back; there were circular motions, then up to my shoulders. His lips dusted my neck, with only the sound of our heavy breathing and the hiss of the water as his hands slowly massaged my shoulders, and then, slowly moving down, under my arms and round to the front, grazing my nipples, slowly moving down in circular motions.

My tears mingled with the water. His touch was so gentle, as it went down, slowly down, until I felt the intimacy of his touch. Our breathing was heavy, and we lingered like this as the water rippled over us. Then, turning me towards him, his lips brushed against mine, kissing me, caressing me as if there was no end. Our arms circled our bodies, and we held on to each other for an eternity. It felt like every muscle in my body was aching, yet relaxing at the same time, until the water cooled.

He took my hand and led me, dripping wet, to the bed. There our bodies embraced, wrapped in each other, wanting every part of each other, exploring a rising passion which we gave to each other. Our bodies totally connected, rising, encircling each other until we reached that peak. Then, afterward, we drifted into a deep sleep, like no other.

❍

Waking up, I found myself alone, wet, relaxed. Surely, that was not it?

As I lay there with my jumbled thoughts about the night before, John walked in, cuddled up with, "Woke up, needed some space to collect my thoughts, needed to come back to prove it was not a dream. I have started a journey and hope you will be with me for it. It won't be easy, but we'll be together. Please think about being with me."

Wanting to understand what might lie ahead, I looked at him. "John—"

"Robbie don't mention the age thing. I know that worries you. Do you like me? See yourself with me always? Think you could love me? Maybe marry me? Just spend the rest of our days together. Or just be a friend? That's all I ask. Age is not an issue for me."

"John, what made you think we could go somewhere?"

Looking at me with an intense smile: "When you called me John, I knew you looked beyond the Johnno."

I saw a man who had opened up his life and his heart to me with total trust. It triggered feelings I had never felt before. I knew we had reached the point of no return.

Fighting back emotion: "John, I have never been happier. Yes, I know I am on the path to falling in love with you. I'm so scared, though. No one has ever wanted me so much; the feelings you show me overwhelm me. I have never wanted to be with anyone so much, but—"

"Robbie, if you think this is puppy love, forget it. I cannot get enough of you. I feel so safe with you. You shield me, comfort me ... hell! I don't know how to express what I feel, but God, it feels good."

Smiling yet again, I knew this was the ignition that started my engine every time.

"Robbie, the shower made me realise that when you are falling in love with someone, it all falls into place."

I wondered if his kisses outdid his smile.

"I understand that, but I am fifty, um plus, but the age thing is still there for me. I have never felt the emotions I am experiencing with you. Hey, please give me time; I'm trying to keep up with you. Okay?"

"Sure, all the time in the world. I can live with that and will give you a lifetime to decide, as long as I'm always there with you. I want to make you happy, care for you, share our lives. Come on sleepy head, it's Sunday, let's take in a movie."

CHAPTER 6

The yellow beast always drew a crowd, and Sunday movies were packed, so we were noticed. I know a lot of people enjoy that, but I have never sought attention; it makes me uneasy. So dark sunnies were the go, but everyone knew who John was. He had experienced it for years and learnt to ignore it.

John is a James Bond fanatic so you can guess the choice of movie. He booked Gold Class, so fewer adoring fans to deal with. But as we left, the lightbulb flashes told us we had not escaped unnoticed. John seemed not to worry. It was almost as if he wanted to bring it on, almost shouting out: 'This is who I want to be with!'

Driving home, I queried with him, and he replied, "What will be, will be." But he hated the fact I had to suffer because of him. Looking at me, he came out with such a caring statement. "If it ever gets too much for you, I will understand if you walk. I will be devastated, Robbie. Now I have found you, but you have a life too. You mean so much to me. I will do everything I can to protect you, to the point of retiring from footy if needs be. I can see a life ahead with you, and that's far more important to me."

"Footy is your life and you are at the peak of your career."

"I thought so too, but since I met you, it is nothing if you are not with me."

"John, being with you means so much to me, too. I see no reason to walk away, so we won't let the bastards win. Old novelists can be tough in their own way—like a war with words—and I can see what we have together. Hit the gas, young man, make the muffler roar!"

John laughed. "You can be a goon sometimes."

By next morning, the photos had circulated with a headline: *Johnno Out with a Much Older Man*. The article went on to discuss this. Are they a couple? Are they flaunting it? Or is it just an old man preying on a star? Probably promoting his book sales as the well-known novelist, Robert Burke, is gay, and so it went on.

Must say though, I liked the 'well-known'.

John had left early, but texted that his family, Footy First, and basically the whole media world was after him. I only had Ruth to contend with who was relishing in it. "Dare I say a potential famous brother-in-law?" *God help us!*

I texted him: "Let us play it cool for a couple weeks. You be seen out alone or with others, and same for me, just until the dust settles."

Texted back: "Hate that."

Texted him: "Relax, let us try it. We can still talk on the phone. I already have media staking out my place. I do not want to tell Ruth; she'd be over here every five minutes in a new outfit."

Texted me: "Okay, hate it, but love you."

Texted him: "Mutual x."

Ruth called; how unusual. "Okay, what's the go, secret service brother?"

"What are you talking about?"

"Oh, just aged gay novelist and spunky Aussie football star at Gold Class movies watching James Bond in action. Hoping to pick up a few martini tips?"

"Just two mates at the movies, Ruth."

"Darling brother, you are joking! Have you read the social media pages, Twitter, and all those? Admit you have some great support from the LGTB plus people, but straight Aussie football fans are not happy."

"Maybe they need to know that John is a man who is entitled to his own life. He shouldn't be expected to live his life just for the benefit of the multitudes of footy fans who want an idol to worship on a pedestal. He has no real life as they sit at home on the couch with chips and a beer. Maybe they need to look in their own backyards. If he retired, it would all go away, and he could get his life back."

"What! That's unbelievable, you'd make him retire?"

"Ruth, as much as I love you, I will pretend I never heard that comment. Few people really know him, but I can assure you, he knows exactly what he wants and no one, not even me, will tell him what to do. You said to me when I first met him, he was a man of few words, but he is an intelligent, caring, thoughtful man and, off the record—trust your beak is glued—a man who makes me feel like the jewel in the crown."

"Fucking novelist! When's the wedding?"

"Bitch."

CHAPTER 7

The next two weeks, for a change, were uneventful. When I went out, the media camp flashed away, and when I came home, even with the groceries, they flashed again. Oh, such riveting stuff. I invited Ruth over for coffee and she was ready for the media, but to her disdain, not one flashbulb.

She arrived, making the comment that it was just because Johnno was not with her. I did not have the heart to tell her whenever I went in or out, the street lit up. Ruth quizzed me as to what was going on, but I felt it was best just to say John was a friend, and he enjoyed talking to me to help him discover where his life was going. Ruth looked at me cynically with, "Oh, yes. Well, I shall leave it at that for the time being and will wait for breaking news. I am sure it will be interesting. Bye secret service man."

A peck on the cheek and out the door to an unlit street. I really should have followed her out, given the waiting photographers wanted something to snap at. It would have made her day.

John rang several times a day, sometimes more often, giving me updates of the media attention and what he said were like dot points in my mind.

- Johnno has gone underground hiding from the old boyfriend.

- No sign of him with the aged novelist (John always got a laugh out of this one). Has he come to his senses and is really looking for the girl of his dreams?
- Definitely realised he is being conned.
- Someone had the nerve to post, "Did we get it wrong and just friends?" Apparently, the journo who said that was shot down for that comment.
- Are his novels worth reading?
- Just so he can write a story and make money like: "I dated and slept with a young football star."

John thought they were all funny, but I hated the way he was treated, like public property, to be derided. They had no idea how his feelings were being hurt, and I knew deep down that he truly hated it. Laughing it off was his mechanism to protect himself.

It was a long two weeks, and I knew deep down we were only putting off what we would continue to endure if our friendship continued. I actually don't think I had any concept, at that time, what the future would deliver us.

So we waited, waited, and waited. Two weeks can be a long time in love land.

Two weeks later, there was a knock on the door. John, all smiles, "Like chocolates?" I was presented with a bouquet of chocolates. I guess they are more edible than traditional roses.

Fortunately, by now, the media camp had become bored and left. He grabbed me, kissing me as if there was no tomorrow. "Gotta make up for lost time, lover. It's time for a drink and a big cuddle, old man."

"Watch it, you might be out on your ear."

"Would you chuck a man onto the street who brought you a bouquet of chocolates?"

Looking at him sternly, "Do not smile."

Straight-faced. "Glad I know your weakness."

I poured some drinks as he spoke. "Seriously, I know I am a liability, but glad you made us do the two weeks. It gave me time to reflect on things. To think about what I really wanted. I know you have been cautious, and I came on too strong, right from the word go. But I've been around long enough to know what I really want.

"I grew up in a straight, testosterone-fuelled world, saw the guys chasing chicks, lust in their eyes, which they thought was important in their lives. Onto the next root, then brag about it. I must be a girl. Why brag about your intimate times with someone special you like or love? Guess they just saw it as a casual root.

"My dad is not the easiest person, as you know. He powered me to where I am, but ignored my brothers because they did not come up to scratch. You know, the one person he idolised, put on a pedestal and would give his life for was Mum. I see him bark at me and my brothers, criticise us, but turn around and show his soft side only to Mum. That is the one good thing he taught me. Always knew I wanted that. Robbie, if I am lucky enough to be your soul mate, and maybe have children with you, our children will be brought up with respect, and I will always be your man."

"Slow down!" I gasped. "Children?! Wow! You need to slow down, young man! I have discovered the good caring side in you, but this blows me away. You are the most extraordinary man I have ever met. Finding you has been really special. You really truly believe in us."

"With your consent, I feel we are working towards something special, and I want to tell my family and Footy First that I am gay. I know now I am. Every time I look at you, I am excited and know deep down how I feel about you. I respect the fact that you need time, which I willingly give you. But whatever happens in the future, I know I am gay, so I need, and want, to issue a statement to clear the air and hopefully ease the media pressure. But I won't make any reference to us. It is early days for us and that is for us to work out away from the spotlight with no pressure on you. You mean so much to me. Will you be there for me in that?"

Looking at him, I said I would, but added that it would open the floodgates. He agreed but asked me if I was ready for that. He told me he would never want to cause me grief, as that would really bring him great sadness.

"John, we are in this together. Bring it on."

He grabbed me, hugged me and cried, as I continued to wonder what lay ahead.

CHAPTER 8

I was excited to get a call from George Raftview, a novelist I admired and had met several times. He was organising a small writer's conference in the Blue Mountains over three days and asked if I would attend and speak, as well as being involved in some workshops. Excitedly, I agreed. He said accommodation would be paid, but we all had to get there under our own steam, which did not worry me. It was a low budget to get new inspiring writers involved. It was great to be included in it.

That night, when John was over for dinner, I told him all about it and said it was a great opportunity for me. He listened intently, but I could see expectation in his eyes.

"John, I will not ask you to come as it will be all work, okay?"

Looking crestfallen, he replied, "Sure, so good for you."

I could see his sadness that he was not to be included, but it made no sense. It was work. I explained I would be tied up in writer's talks all the time and each night at the dinners.

No smile.

"John, spit it out. I know you well by now, okay?"

"Robbie, do you want a break from me?"

Looking at this man I had come to know so well, strong in body, but with the softest heart, I knew I held his love in my hands.

"John, it's my work, like your training. We both need to do those things, and our relationship needs to take those things into account. Our love doesn't diminish because we are apart. Will you drive me to the airport and pick me up on return?"

His happy nature returned. "Can I wait in the car park for three days?" I got a smile.

The conference date came around quickly, with John dropping me off at the airport. I sat in a bar sipping a drink. In some respects, I was looking forward to some 'me' time surrounded by words. Relationships can be wonderful, but now and then, a little space helps. John is a passionate man and I feel him with me all the time. Not complaining, but yes, we all need a little space to gather our thoughts.

After the flight, I noticed three missed calls from John. What was that about space?

I rang; it was good to hear his voice. He asked about the trip; had I met the others yet? I sensed he did not want to get off the phone. We ended the call, and I felt down and knew he felt the same. I rang back and got message bank so left, "Love you."

A minute later, he rang. "Thanks, I needed that. Sorry, I must drive you mad. I will leave you alone now."

"Never. We know what we are to each other; I'm off to the first dinner."

"Good, enjoy, watch out for all those sexy writers," he hung up with a laugh.

I enjoyed the dinner, drinks, and writers' chat over dinner. I needed to tell John there were no sexy writers, although there were curious delegates who were interested in what charm I possessed to score the famous 'Johnno'. Can we ever escape? I wonder how many people out there still love someone for who they are and not the famous side of them. I had seen up close how John had to deal with it and how it impacted on our lives. I guess it will never go away. Maybe there's a novel in it!

The conference stimulated my creativity, and I knew I needed to do more. I loved the life John and I were creating, but we still needed to continue to develop our own interests. That would keep the relationship fertile and stimulate its growth. For the first time in my life, I saw a rosy future. I looked forward each evening to the calls from John. Despite that, for some reason, I did not sleep well. It was no fun finding an empty pillow beside me in the morning.

Upon my return, as I waited in the pick-up zone, I recognised Ginge's four-wheel drive coming towards me. My heart sank until I saw John at the wheel. "All okay, John?"

"Yes, I know you hate the attention the yellow beast causes, so this is a surprise to welcome my man home."

I climbed in and we sped off. We made small talk until we walked through my door, dropping the luggage as our arms surrounded each other. "John, I did miss you. I hated seeing that empty pillow in the morning. I didn't sleep well each night, just so good to be back with you."

He hugged me so much. "Was the same for me, Robbie. I worry about you not getting any sleep at your age, better get you straight to bed." He always knew how to hit that button.

At some stage we woke up with the house in darkness. Curled up, I kissed him with, "I've been asked to go to another conference in Melbourne for five days."

He gave me a quizzical look. "But after this last one, I know I need someone to carry my bags."

"Well, I just think I might be strong enough to carry them for you, old man."

"You know you get a spanking if you call me old."

"Good to know a man you can rely on." He knew not to smile.

CHAPTER 9

John has played some of the toughest games in his career, but nothing had prepared him for the meeting with his parents and brothers. It had to happen; he knew. His journey had started, and he wanted it to continue. He had made a life choice and being with me had opened his eyes to a relationship that liberated him, so he knew he had to be true to himself; he had to walk this path.

Explaining all of this to his family was something he was not looking forward to. He had asked me how I told my parents; how did they react?

I explained it was in a time much less liberated than now, and it was not easy for them. It was difficult to tell extended family and friends—there was a shadow of shame in those days. I guess to a certain extent it is still there today with some people. Fortunately for me, Ruth took charge when the revelation occurred. I have always had her support.

So came the moment of truth.

John's family sat around the table with cups of tea. Hey, maybe something stronger was really needed? His dad challenged him, "What you got to say that's so important?"

"Well, Mum, Dad, Tony, Ginge. You have seen all the recent press about me."

"Yeah, that dirty old bloke leading you on; should be locked up."

Silence.

"Actually, if you must know, it is me who is leading him on."

"Bet he put you up to say that! What hold has he got over you? We can sort him out. Blokes like that need that now and then."

"Dad, that is so gross. Everyone can see how happy Johnno is. Let him be." John looked at Ginge, "Thanks, mate."

"Go for it, Johnno, not my thing, but glad you got the guts," and Ginge walked out.

John looked at his mother, Merryl, and older brother, Tony, for support. Their faces were expressionless.

John stood up. "I cannot believe I'm hearing my own father say this. Sort him out. I am gay. I chased him and want him. He resisted me, yes, resisted me. Can you hear that? Tried to turn me away, but I wouldn't let him, and if you must know, I would end my footy career today to get out of this continuous media torture, to be with him for the rest of my life.

"What does the famous Johnno Willadoro have to show for his life up to now? A bright yellow Maserati and adoring fans who at night go home to loved ones. But little Johnno is expected to play on the field again and again, to entertain them. Yes, that's just what it is, entertainment! Am I entitled to have a life with a partner? Hope so. Dad, you are a tough man, but you love, respect, and would do anything for Mum. I grew up seeing that and that's what I want too."

"She's a woman!"

"Well, sometimes it doesn't always work out that way. I love a man. A man who has all the qualities you could hope for in a partner. Sure, our ages are different, but that's like race, religion, hair colour, and the rest. You need to follow your heart."

"Don't know who taught you all this crap you say. You didn't learn it here in this house."

"No, Dad, I didn't learn a lot of things here, but I'm learning now. The man I love has been subjected to the most vicious torment. I cannot believe he puts up with it for me, but if you had the decency to understand him, you might understand why. I thought I could make you understand, but I see it is pointless. That is so sad, Dad. I love you as my dad, but I don't understand you as my dad. Have you any concept that I might want to be happy in my life?"

"Do you want to be known forever as a 'poof'? You have a fabulous footy career that is the envy of everyone. Money and girls, they fall at your feet! Pity you didn't pick one up now and then."

"Have you ever tried taking all that crap home at night and curling up in bed with it?"

"You got a fantastic car."

"Dad, everyone knows Maserati's are dud sex."

"Just excuses."

"Yes, Dad, excuses for a life. I intend to spend the rest of my life with Robbie, if he will have me, with or without your blessing. I now see no point in punishing you all anymore. If need be, I will consider retirement from the game."

CHAPTER 10

After the showdown with his family, John had a meeting with Footy First. Later that day, he told me how it went. The directors and management were not happy with the publicity. They spoke strongly to John that he should kerb this friendship with the older man and put out a statement he was just a family friend. He should also say he was looking forward to marriage and that he had several lady friends who were in his eye.

He told them all that was a lot of bullshit, and they needed to understand he was gay, end of story.

The discussion became heated to the point he yelled at them: "If you don't like it, sack me, tear up my contract, and take the fucking car back. I'm gay, end of story. Haven't I always played a fair game? I've never done anything wrong, never brought the club into disrepute. I've kept a low profile and denied myself a personal relationship during my whole career! Do you people understand the gender issues that are happening out there in the real world? People are standing up for their right to happiness."

Producing a sheet of paper, he threw it on the table. "If you want me to stay, issue this without any changes." And he just walked out.

Footy First issued a statement to the press.

The following is a personal statement from Mr Johnno Willadoro:

> *I have been shocked by the statements that have been circulating in all social and media outlets about me. To put an end to speculation, although it should be a personal issue for me alone, I am gay. No further discussion is needed.*
>
> *As a gay man, I hope, with the support of my teammates, I can continue to play and represent the country I love. Time will tell.*
>
> *Statements have been made that I have been seen in the company of a man older than me. These are true, and we have been always seen in public places, and never tried to hide it. He is a valued friend who has been helping me through what I am finding a difficult period of my life. Most people are allowed these moments in private.*
>
> *My friend has been subjected to the most relentless abuse in social media. I have told him I would understand if he turned his back on me. He has told me that he wanted to support me through this difficult period and that we needed to prove what we always believed about our country, that everybody gives their mates a fair go. Both of us have been given tremendous support by our families and friends.*
>
> *Thank you.*

Footy First had no input into this statement and will make no further comment.

Later, as I sat alone on the veranda, John walked out with two drinks. We sat in silence, clinked glasses and he murmured, "Well, I've given them more fodder to chew over. You reckon it will ever end?"

Even for me, it was hard to say. The juggernaut of social media, Twitter, as well as all the print and electronic media, gave everyone a voice. I remember discussing this with my dad, who had been a journalist all his life, when he said in his day, the press respected people's personal lives. Times have changed.

"John, we always knew it would not be easy, but we have made a commitment to each other. That bond is strong. Hey what's that saying? 'Slings and arrows' ... Is the glass in the Maserati tough?"

He laughed. "Probably but won't stop Twitter.'

CHAPTER 11

After the media frenzy of John's public announcement, he rang and suggested a day at the beach. He'd heard of a beach south of Byron Bay, in New South Wales, where you could discreetly skinny dip. He said he wanted to do that with me. I commented to him that I was not at an age to be out in my nylon swimmers. This resulted in a retort, "I've seen it all, but still want more."

He suggested we drive to Bryon Bay the day before, have dinner, stay over, and spend the next day at the beach. Agreeing, I suggested I could do a picnic, but he insisted we would buy food there, as it was going to be a break for me.

"Robbie, we will wear big floppy hats, even bigger sunglasses, so no one will know we are there. Okay, lover?"

"Okay, young man, hard to resist you."

As we lay on the beach, I reflected on how my life had changed. It was almost too good to be true, in fact. John himself seemed too good to be true, but I always saw in his eyes the care and love he felt for me. No doubts, but just a concern for the future.

We swam together naked, midweek, no one around, and the water was cool. John held me, saying he would keep me warm. However, I knew at the back of our minds, we both wondered if anyone was hiding in the bushes with a camera. Sad how that is always with you; we loved it when we closed the doors on the world.

"Robbie, you think what I'm thinking?"

"Yes; glad we walked in wearing sarongs?" He smiled a very cheeky smile.

"They make nice belts in the water," and laughed.

We enjoyed our time in the water, two lovers, enjoying the intimacy of touch. Dripping wet, we walked up the beach in sarongs.

"Robbie, you always speak of your love of going to Ubud in Bali. Will you take me?"

"Of course, I would love that very much. You say when as I know you have your commitments."

"Well, the footie season finishes in two weeks. There'll be some dinners to celebrate, which I hate, then after the 25th of the month would be great."

"Okay, I will book a villa, and look at flights."

"Business class is on me, just to keep us away from the fans, okay?"

"Okay, but you still realise we will be in the public eye."

"I'm over it all. Just book, and if you can cope with it, I certainly can. Time for a life. Just love being with you, but I worry a lot about what it does to you."

"Together, we can deal with it. Penestanan on the outskirts of Ubud is quieter, so no one will know you, sorry."

"Sounds like heaven to me," he chuckled.

CHAPTER 12

As Ruth drove us to the airport, John clutched my hand. We knew we were putting ourselves in the limelight with a trip like this, but we had agreed we needed to get on with our lives.

Checking in, security and passport control went well, but we knew eyes were on the two of us. Fortunately, cameras were banned in those areas.

We headed straight for the airline lounge, which gave us some security. We checked with the young guy at the lounge reception as to the latest time we could board, to enable us to be the last to embark. Winking, he commented, "I will alert the stewards. You will be last on. My friend Jason is working business class. He'll look after you."

I looked at a perplexed John and smiled, saying, "Family."

At the boarding gate, we were told to wait. Our concern quickly turned to surprise as we were surreptitiously escorted on by Jason, straight into business class, unseen by all the other passengers.

"Settle in guys. Don't need any sticky beaks, do we now? What would you like to drink?"

"Bubbles, thank you."

"Thought so."

After touchdown, we were met by an arrival service that discreetly collected us straight away. They took us through immigration and organised our bags to be collected. We then cleared customs without being spotted once.

Ketut, the driver who had collected me for so many visits to Bali, was waiting for us. He brought me up to date with all the news about his family and invited us both to his home during our visit.

I told him we didn't need to do tourist things, but I had to take John whitewater rafting on the river I had been on before. I also explained that I wanted to book a day tour of some important cultural areas I had done before with a friend.

We pulled out of the airport, and I knew John was in for a surprise. "The traffic, Robbie, it's ballistic!"

Every vehicle, motorbike, scooter, and hand-pushed cart you could imagine was weaving its way at various speeds along the road. I watched John's face; his mouth was open.

"This is insane!"

Laughing, I said, "Remember you said to me, 'Robbie, let's hire a motorbike and ride down country roads'?"

Shaking his head, he announced, "Let's stick with Ketut."

Winding through the traffic for over an hour-and-a-half, John was fascinated with everything he saw. Talk about opening a boy's eyes. He had never been to Asia before, so it was a real experience.

Arriving at our destination, John fell in love with the villa. "I want to be in the pool with you," he said.

"Should we unpack? No, stuff that!" He pulled off my clothes and we jumped into the cooling water, hugging and kissing. John shouted out, arms outstretched, "Eat your heart out, Twitter".

He kissed me slowly with, "I want a family with you." My hug answered him.

After we settled into a peaceful routine, I told John I wanted to take him to explore some of the traditional culture of the island. Having done a similar day trip several times before, I knew what would give him a taste of old Bali.

We headed off with Ketut at the wheel, fortunately navigating all the traffic around us, to the Klungkung Royal Palace, officially called Puri Agung Semarapura, which is a historic building situated in Semarapura. It is the capital of the Klungkung Regency and established in the 17th century. All that remains today is the Hall of Justice decorated with unique paintings done in the Kamasan style.

Being his first exposure to Asia, Ketut's explanation of the history of the building and the paintings captivated John. His phone clicked away, capturing endless images of the exotic paintings.

Then we moved on, swallowed up by the traffic and arriving at a special place in my heart—Tirta Gangga; this is a former royal palace in eastern Bali, about five kilometres from Karangasem, near Abang. The Hindu name for the sacred River Ganges, Tirta Gangga, is noted for the Karangasem royal water palace, bathing pools and its Patirthan Temple.

"Gee, Robbie, one surprise after another."

We quietly wandered over the stepping stones, trying not to fall in, while John enjoyed feeding all the fish. He turned into a boy for the day.

No place was too far away, but the traffic slowed us. After the two stops and winding up the mountains, we arrived high in the hills for lunch at one of the tourist buffet restaurants overlooking Mount Agung. It was a spectacular spot.

Mount Agung, an active volcano, is a very sacred Balinese landmark and is home to one of Bali's most important temples, Pura Besakih, known as the Mother Temple. Situated high on the slopes of the mountain, the temple holds deep cultural significance. Worshiped by the Balinese, locals believe that Mount Agung is the abode of the gods.

Being a buffet lunch with food in *bain maries,* I suggested the best dishes for John to choose, so as to save any nasty gastric issues down the track. A cold Bintang beer went down well. We sat there after lunch, with another Bintang, enjoying time out with no footy fans. Silly, but it was so important for us. John beamed at me. "This is the best time, Robbie; we are going to make life happen for us."

After lunch, we motored on to a temple for John to experience the heart of local life. I had been to the Hindu temple of Pura Kehen several times before and liked it. It had fewer tourists, though the locals were always there performing their spiritual rituals.

John was not sure about wearing a sarong in public to enter the temple, but I told him he would soon love wearing one at home. I reminded him he had a taste of a sarong at Byron. Now, this was the real experience.

At the end of the day, Ketut shared a drink with us at the villa and we planned the whitewater rafting day. Later, we wandered down to a family eatery called 'Sri Uma' for a *nasi campur*. I discovered John was enjoying the local food; he wanted to work through the menu. We were just two men, sharing a meal together, laughing, happy in a local *Warung*, with nobody taking any notice of us except saying, "Hi," as they passed by. I could see my man was in heaven.

Next day, our room boy, Dewar, prepared fresh fruit, and scrambled eggs for breakfast, as he did each morning. I suggested a walk into town via the rice fields—well, the few that were left in the area—for lunch in town, if John felt he could cope.

"Book it Robbie. As I said, it's time for living."

I knew a great restaurant in an old, converted warehouse which was always popular.

So, we walked into town, hats and sunnies, like James Bond undercover. Such fun!

Arriving for lunch, we were taken upstairs, which was crowded. As we sat down, minus hats and sunnies, we felt eyes on us. However, we ignored everyone and just ordered our drinks. I suggested a gin and tonic, as I thought we might need it.

We perused the menu, and I could see John frowning; he had no idea about any of the dishes.

"John, shall I order?"

He nodded with great relief. We settled into a delightful grazing lunch of slipper lobster dumplings with padang style chilli sauce and fried curry leaf; beef sate padang with thick curry sauce served with rice cake and pickled vegetables; crispy whole fish rice paddy tilapia served with two traditional sambals—ikan asin manis and sambal mango; and hand chopped duck salad with snake bean, roasted coconut, palm heart, sambal telur, and semanggi. After all, it was just lunch. He actually loved it.

As we got up to go, another diner rushed over and told John he was a great fan. The guy asked for a selfie with John. Concerned for our privacy, John sought my approval, but I nodded and offered to take the photo. It was a great shot, giving the fan a happy memory to take home.

Then, an extraordinary thing happened. As we left the restaurant, everyone burst into applause. John waved to them, and cheers erupted. The applause and cheers gave us hope of approval.

Leaning into my ear, John nudged me. "Geez, Robbie, I need a beer after that. Do you think the tide is turning?"

"I hope so."

While in Bali, a few, no, let's-get-real, thousands of photos—including the selfie—erupted in the media thanks to helpful tourists. But for once, some of the comments were kind. I still got called the 'old man'. John liked that; he said it showed he had good taste. I gave him the novelist look, but that didn't dim his smile.

There was also a plethora of texts and emails from home. We let family know we would talk on return and John sent an email to Footy First saying he would meet with them after his holiday.

Next day, we had planned a whitewater rafting trip, and despite the lunch hiatus, decided to go regardless. I mean, how many more photos could be taken? Millions, I guess. Fortunately, the majority were amateurs, so most were blurred.

Ketut picked us up and mentioned he had seen lots of photos on social media about us. He queried why. I explained who John was, though because he didn't follow Aussie football, he laughed.

Arriving at the departure point on the Ayung River, we were given life jackets and helmets, but nobody took any notice of us other than polite "Hellos." We seemed to be ignored. Maybe it was because we had struck a Chinese tour group who were ignorant about Australian football. What a lucky day for us. We were nobodies!

The raft took off and John was a young boy again, quickly joining our fellow passengers, yelling and screaming as we jettisoned down the river, crashing into rocks, avoiding or riding out the rapids. We became drenched with water as we passed under waterfalls. That didn't stop John from giving lots of excuses to hold me, ostensibly saving me from falling out. There were no complaints from me.

It opened our eyes to spectacular views of unspoiled rainforest and rice fields, together with amazing stone carvings on some areas of the river walls. The carvings depicted the story of Ramayana, an important Hindu epic which traces the life of Prince Rama, marriage, exile, and travels.

It was a special time together. So few we have ever experienced together in public. We arrived at the end of the rapids wet, happy, and relaxed. It was very special.

That night was our last. We had ordered our favourite food—*nasi campur*—to be delivered. We sat on the edge of the pool naked, drinking Bintang beer. We were so sad it was our last night together in Penestanan, but I assured John it would not be our last.

Despite the wonderful time we had been having, John seemed nervous, anxious about something. After all this time together, I could read him. I queried this; he said he had something to share with me. He had been mulling over it for some time, and more so all week. He wanted to be sure of it in his mind before talking.

That was when he blurted out to me it was all over. I was shocked.

He saw the anguish in my face and grabbing me, he hugged and kissed me, saying, "NO, no, not us! Football!"

He explained that he had reached the point when he needed to move on.

"Robbie, I have given my life so far to football and the fans. I'm not giving you to them. We have a life to get on with."

In his mind, he knew it was time. Our relationship was going from strength to strength, but the overwhelming intrusion by the media made him anxious and he wanted to put a stop to that. He knew it intruded ... no, it violated my life, and his love of the game had gone sour because of it.

"We have a future and I want us to build on that. In fact, I have a plan to share with you."

John had been very diligent using the money he earnt in selecting prime real estate, which had increased in value. He saw a career in real estate, and I could see the excitement building up in him as he talked about it.

"I have it all planned out, but just wanted it all clear in my head before I said anything to you." He was sure all his footy contacts would be there for him. "We are in this together."

I observed a man creating a new beginning. Kissing, we fell into bed. Dinner was still sitting there untouched in the morning.

❍

We arrived home to an explosion of media flashes. Surely, they would get bored with us one day?

Ruth was waiting, and we bundled into the car, speeding off. Home in one piece. Glad we didn't bother taking any holiday photos. Everyone else did it for us.

The press, every media outlet, influencer, social media platform had turned into a feeding frenzy. Our break away had been reduced to a grubby escapade. John ignored it and said it only made him adamant in his resolve to retire.

The night after we got back, he came for dinner, his arrival lighting up the street. He walked in and found me weeping; a flashlight army camped outside for the last few days had drained me. I felt my life was being torn apart. My every move outside was captured, my privacy stripped away. I had purposely not read any of the media postings. John held me in his arms, cradled me, as I wept.

"Robbie, if it helps, there have been some great supportive posts and not just from the LGTBQ community. Some prominent media people have slammed the treatment we have received, saying it was an appalling indictment on the media. Looking me straight in the eyes, Robbie. Is it getting too much for you?"

"No," I sighed. "I just needed to let some emotions out, and with your support, I will be okay. I guess I worry you are retiring more for me than yourself."

He kissed me for a long time. "No more talk like that, Robbie. I'm doing this for us, but I will admit that I am really looking forward to it. A new career that will be exciting for me and with you by my side, that's the true bonus."

I knew we were still on that same path.

CHAPTER 13

John resolved there was no turning back. He met with Footy First and resigned. He told them he would make a public statement.

The media room at the hotel was crammed. Media people of all types were there, as well as every news outlet, photographers, video cameras, and, of course, the media team from Footy First. The air was filled with an electric pulse as it had been announced that the star boy, Johnno Willadoro, would speak; no questions would be allowed. Rumours were rife as to content.

Suddenly, there was a hush as Roger Brown, the CEO, entered, followed by an obviously nervous Johnno. As they faced the media throng, Johnno's eyes scanned the room and his eyes fixed on me briefly in the back corner. I could see him visibly relax and smiled at the room.

After being introduced, he shot me a quick glance and started. His words were strong and firm and spoken with such determination. I was proud of him.

> *I issued a statement some time ago and have been shocked by the reports that have continued to circulate in all press media and social media outlets. It has been relentless, but my friend and I have been pleased with the incredible support shown to us by so*

> *many people out there. Sadly, this has been overshadowed by the vitriol levelled against us.*
>
> *As a gay man, I had hoped I could continue to play and represent the country I love. This is not to be, and today, with regret, I handed in my resignation.*
>
> *I wish my team mates well, and that the team continues to grow in the future.*
>
> *My friend and I have endured relentless social media harassment. I hope this may cause some to reflect on the hurt that can be caused to those of us who are not perceived as 'fitting the mould'.*
>
> *I state publicly to my friend, the man I now proudly call my partner, I could not have survived this period without his unwavering support, and that of those close to us. I am a very fortunate man.*
>
> *Thank you for your time.*

He looked up and smiled at me. Then, he quickly turned, and walked out. By the time the room turned to see who he smiled at, they found an empty corner.

I waited silently in the back seat of the car. John climbed in, saying to the driver, "Please drive."

As the car pulled out, he took my hand, and looking straight ahead, he wept. I gripped his hand while we drove in silence.

I let him have these moments, then he cheekily turned to me, "Shall we get dropped off at the nearest church and make a real day of it?"

Chuckling, we held our tongues; we had learnt we were only secure behind closed doors. As the car pulled up at the hotel, John thanked the driver, who replied, "You blokes got my vote."

Walking into the hotel, I kept my distance from John. While we waited for the lift, John took my hand. Finally, in the lift, he gazed into my eyes and stated, "I feel an incredible weight lifted."

We entered our room, fell into a hug, and sobbed. Our phones were exploding as we dropped onto the bed and fell into a deep sleep.

When we awoke, John opened a bottle of Moet. "Let's see if we made the news!"

"You are joking."

The news had started, and we saw the tail end of John's speech before the newsreader crossed to Parliament House.

"Well," I said, "looks like no comments. Guess that's a plus."

The Prime Minister appeared and spoke: "I am a great football fan and I believe in fair play. Johnno Willadaro epitomises the very best in sport. He is a true Australian legend. I watched his statement today and I say to you, my admiration for this man holds no bounds. He spoke from the heart with honesty, and I say to you, my fellow Australians, we should be supportive of him and the partner of his choice. He upholds the true essence of mateship. Go well boys."

John turned the TV off, and we sat in silence.

"John," I said, "If you ever thought you had doubts in yourself, you can forget them now. I am so proud of you, and proud to be your partner."

He gazed at me, just that smile, and kissed me.

"Robbie, we are partners in life."

We clinked glasses and crawled into bed. What a day!

As we curled up, he stared lovingly at me. "Will you marry me?"

I was stunned into silence.

"Well? What? I'm hanging here for an answer; I'm on tenterhooks here."

"No one has ever asked me that. No one will ever again." I felt exultant. "Yes! You are the only one.".

We fell into each other's arms and woke up the next morning feeling on top of the world for the first time in ages.

I rolled over and, looking at him announced, "I think you need to move in."

He hugged me. "My bags are already packed."

CHAPTER 14

We called on Ruth and family to tell them we were getting married.

Ruth was beside herself; Jimmy was excited to have Johnno in the family, even if he was no longer the star footy player. Barry was cordial, as usual. Perhaps we should have asked him to give Tony Willadoro some lessons. We explained they could tell no one, stressing to Jimmy, he was not to even tell his mates on pain of death. We told everyone we did not want the news to end up as a media circus.

"So, let's plan reception places," said Ruth.

"No, Ruth, no reception house."

Our intention was that only they and John's family knew. No one else was to be told. We would have a barbeque at a new house John had found, which we were in the process of buying, together.

"Secret two at work again," chipped in Ruth.

John and I had a plan; I would deal with my family, and he would cope with his. Guess it was sort of working.

"Ruth, every couple has a right to privacy." Her face said it all.

"As I said, a barbie, both families invited, plus a few close friends, ostensibly for John's birthday. A friend of mine is a marriage celebrant, and we have had some discussions with her. Hopefully, the media will not get wind of it, so we rely on you and John's family to keep quiet about it."

"I cannot tell you all how proud and excited I am that Robbie has agreed to marry me," John declared. "You are all so lucky to have him in your family. I promise I will care for him always."

Ruth cried. Barry and Jimmy shook our hands.

After visiting his family to tell them about our wedding plans, John walked in and poured us a drink in silence. We sat down, clinked glasses, and he looked at me forlornly.

"John, deep breath. Just relax and take your time."

John played out how it went.

"Everyone, time to talk. Robbie and I are really getting on well, and more than that, we want to be together always, so I have asked him to marry me."

Silence.

"Okay, well, I want to share my life with him and hopefully have a family. I know you don't understand Dad, but I love you as my dad and I want you to understand that I will only be happy if he is in my life."

"Only bring you grief. You will go down in history as a disgraced footy pansy."

"Dad, that is gross. Don't you see how happy I am with him?"

"No, he's just an old man preying on a young boy."

"You're joking Dad! Am I a young boy at twenty-eight? Robbie has never said a thing against any of you; he's always friendly to you on the few occasions you have met, yet you treat him like shit, except Ginge," John added, looking at his mum and Tony for any support. However, they remained silent.

He continued. "I would not be the man I am today without him. He looks for nothing but my love, which I give freely to him because he is the first person, yes—person of any gender or sexuality whatsoever—to unconditionally love me, be my support, my strength.

"I wake up every morning and want him to be beside me. His love is boundless, so I want to share my life with him as my partner, husband, and hopefully we can have children together. Please, Dad, be there for us. I want you all part of our family."

His dad stood up, walked out and left with a comment over his shoulder, "Make a mess of your life if you want."

John walked outside and turned to look back at the house that had been his home since he was born. It looked foreign now. As he was about to get in the car, he saw his mum and Ginge come out onto the veranda. Expecting possibly a wave, but there was none, he saw they were deep in conversation before they turned and walked back inside.

Throughout our discussion, I tried to reassure him that it would take time with his dad. But a despondency had sabotaged his happiness, and there was no smile for me.

We sat there, drink in hand, when John's phone rang.

"Ginge, what's up?" I watched him listening and his face showed surprise. "Okay, thanks Ginge," and he hung up.

He looked emotional, so I waited until he could speak. "Mum asked Ginge to ring me. He was to tell me that, as I know, she always shops Wednesdays at her local shopping centre and has a coffee first at 10 am at The Sunshine Coffee Shop. She hoped one Wednesday I might buy her a coffee. Can you believe that?"

"Oh, John. I am so pleased for you. Your family are just having trouble dealing with this. It must be a Titanic for them."

"Won't sleep a wink until next Wednesday."

I looked at him. "Oh, no."

❍

Wednesday did arrive, and he had slept.

I watched him drive off in his SUV; the beast was put down after he resigned, he was so pleased.

I settled at my desk, and hours later, he burst in all smiles, cradling the biggest bunch of chocolates.

"Wow, tell me all."

"We hugged as we greeted, then sat and ordered coffee. She told me she had never lied or been secretive with my dad, however she needed to take charge. He was a good, caring man, but my news shook him for six. Never in all their life together had she seen him so bewildered and lost.

"She told me that meeting with me was the first step. She felt he could not be forced into changing his mind, but she was encouraging him in gentle, relaxed situations so that she might ease him into understanding. Mum looked at me, tearfully saying our family now was a devastating sadness for her. She was determined to repair the fracture. I don't think I had ever realised her strength."

"To be honest, she gave me the impression of 'watch this space'."

"What do you think she will do?"

"Not sure, but she had a look of determination."

"After coffee, I helped Mum do her shopping; it took me back to when I often went with her. Told her I had to go down the choccy aisle. She smiled and said, "Is he a sweet tooth?"

"I cannot wait to meet her."

"It may be sooner than you think. Guess what, Mum told me when I was born, and names were discussed she wanted John, but Dad wanted Johnno. He announced he was going to make me into a famous footballer, so he needed a name that stands out. John is suburban. Mum said she was elated when she heard you called me John."

Little did we know that Tony, his dad, was being exposed to numerous comments about John out in the business world.

CHAPTER 15

With football behind John, a wedding to plan, a career to map out, we found ourselves snowed under. John was adamant that there had to be 'us' times, so an occasional trip to Byron Bay was included. But more often, we visited our favourite beach, Alexandra Headland (or Alex, as we sometimes called it), on the Sunshine Coast.

John was in the process of setting up his real estate agency in Toowong. He had asked Todd, a footy mate who was the only one he kept in touch with after his resignation, to join him after the football season. They had always been friends and Todd made it clear to John his 'coming out' would not affect their friendship. The two of them started the course that allowed them to become registered real estate agents.

John had been introduced to a friend's father who was an agent in Toowong and had a sole practice. The father offered John a job with the idea that John would buy the practice when he retired, which was soon. Having a mentor who had been in the business for many years, and who had a great reputation, was a bonus for John. He was happy for Todd to come on board when he retired from the game.

So, my man was busy with his studies. I got back to the two novels I had underway, so the trips up to the coast were a welcome treat, although they often started late Saturday after open houses and auctions. We treated ourselves by coming back early Tuesday morning.

I could see that John was completely engrossed in his new job. Needless to say, there was a lot of real estate talk in the house. He was just like a boy with a new toy.

In between work and studies, John and I had been discussing children; he was eager for a family of our own. We discussed surrogacy, but neither of us was keen on that. We read about mixing both sperms but felt there was always a third party in the picture. So, adoption became the hottest topic in our household. We wanted to help someone who needed a home and was without parents for whatever reason. This was something we felt positive about.

Ruth, Ginge, and his wife, Maureen, did not see it that way. When we had told them we wanted a family and were investigating adoption, this prompted quite a few discussions. They all expressed the view that consideration needed to be given to the issue that two dads may make things difficult for any child growing up. Maureen knew a couple of lesbians with two children, and they got hell at school from other kids. The debate went on and they conceded surrogacy would be a better option if we proceeded. John and I did not see the difference.

One day, Ruth said bluntly, "At least they would have family blood." John and I were deeply hurt by all this and explained again, that we would consider all options.

Not daunted, we made an appointment after completing the volume of online forms and presented ourselves to Clare at the Queensland Adoption Services in Brisbane.

Clare was a straight to the point woman, so we settled comfortably into conversation with her. She was upfront with us that my age was against us. I felt immediately for John and saw the disappointed look that crept over his face. Probably for the first time, my age had rocked us at the core of our relationship.

Knowing what I felt, John took my hand and squeezed it and with a smile—not his best—but still, a smile. Although the same sex relationship was not an issue for the adoption agency, if there were family members to be considered in the adoption process, she had seen negative attitudes in the past. We stated we intended to marry, but she made no comment.

Clare said apart from these issues, nothing else stood in our way. "I want to give you hope; however, I feel a baby is out of the question. You would make ideal parents in the eyes of our agency. At times, we get children who are older, say two, five, or older. How do you feel about that?"

We exchanged glances. John then grinned at us both. "Always wondered how I would deal with the nappies." Looking at me, he recovered that smile. "Robbie?"

"I think that would be good for us."

"Great guys! I would love to see a child placed with you; they would be lucky to have such great dads. Johnno, I followed your story ... my husband was a fan, and I was amazed how you both weathered those times again and again. Meeting you, I now understand. Fingers crossed. I shall be in touch, and soon I hope."

We walked out and found a coffee shop.

"John, my age, I'm sorry."

He could see my eyes well up. Taking my hands, he squeezed them.

"It's a blessing. As I said, no nappies! Always a silver lining." He hugged me. "I know it will happen."

CHAPTER 16

John was quite excited when Todd told him some of the boys from his old team wanted to catch up for a drink at the pub. It had been some months since John had retired, and no one had reached out since, except Todd. I dropped him off and he said he would ring when he was ready to leave but couldn't see it going past midnight. I settled in for a quiet evening but became a little concerned when midnight came and went. I rang him, but my message went to voice mail.

About half an hour later, my phone rang; it was John's phone but an unknown voice. "Robbie, it's Todd on Johnno's phone. There's been an incident here at the pub and Johnno has been taken by ambulance to hospital. The police have arrived."

My heart jumped. "What!" I yelled.

"He's at the Smithfield Road Emergency Hospital."

I was shaking. What the hell was happening?! I called a taxi; I couldn't drive. My whole body was shivering; I think I was in shock. The taxi seemed to take forever.

"Someone sick?" the cabbie asked.

"I hope not." I ran into the hospital and was immediately aware of a police presence. My heart raced. I asked for Johnno Willadoro at reception but was told no such person was there. I was baffled, so I asked them to check again. No, he was not there.

A voice beside me said, "Can I help you, sir?"

I was face-to-face with the police. "I am Detective Sergeant Patrick O'Reilly."

"I am looking for my partner who is supposed to be here, John. Oh! Johnno Willadoro. I'm his partner Robert Burke."

"Yes, Mr Burke, we heard you were coming. Follow me."

"What?"

"I will take you up to the fourth floor. When we discovered who he was, we decided to keep the press at bay."

As we entered the lift, he continued, "Young guys get up to all sorts of things when away from partners. Don't want the press to get on to it, do we? Be a tasty treat for them."

"What do you mean by that remark?" My voice choked with worry. "Is he okay? What happened? Why is he here in hospital with the police about? I need to know now, and your inference is offensive. You don't even know him."

He peered at me quizzically. "Leave the police work to us, sir."

"I need to see him now!" I felt I was about to explode.

"Oh, here is the doctor now. Doctor Hasid, this is Mr Willadoro's partner, Robert Burke."

We shook hands, and the doctor said, "His blood pressure is coming down and he should be awake soon. We have run some tests; he had Rohypnol in his blood, apart from alcohol. The alcohol level was not high."

"No, he's not a big drinker, doctor. But this Rohypnol, I don't understand; what is it?"

"It's commonly called a date rape drug; a tranquiliser about ten times more potent than Valium."

I sank into the chair. I knew another nightmare had begun.

The policeman interrupted. "That is the subject, Mr Burke, of our investigations. I can say no more. Go get a coffee and hopefully the doctor can tell you more soon."

"God, I hope so. What a nightmare. I need to ring my sister and his family. I will leave his family to you. His father will be on the warpath."

Babbling, I rang Ruth, who said Barry would drop her off. I told her to come to the fourth floor as the hospital was silent about John's presence there.

I collected myself. Because it was late and I didn't need abuse from his father, I rang Ginge instead of his dad and explained the little I knew. He said they would come over straight away. He quizzed me about what was happening, but I said no one was telling me anything.

I sat down, totally drained. *The attacks ... will they never go away? Why?* I guess, deep down, I knew.

The policeman walked over. "Tell me what happened tonight, Mr Burke?"

"You can call me Robbie."

"John went out with a footy mate Todd to the pub. I had dropped him off and arranged for him to ring me when ready. He thought it would be no later than midnight. Todd had rung him and said some of the guys from footy days wanted to catch up with him for a drink. He was surprised; no one had made any contact since he retired, and he felt they all wanted to avoid him. I rang him just after twelve and went to voice mail, so I left a message. Shortly after that, Todd rang and said to get over to the Emergency Hospital on Smithfield Road as John had been taken there, and the police were involved. As you would appreciate, I was worried sick and still am."

"Does he often go out like that?"

"No, never! Nobody from footy days ever contacted him."

"Does he think you prefer him to have no contact with them?"

"You don't know him."

"I want to get to the facts of what he got up to at the pub."

I froze. I knew what it was like to have no one on your side.

He looked at me in that quizzical manner he seemed to have. "I cannot say much as it is under investigation, but I can tell you our line of enquiry led us to believe several assaults took place."

"Several assaults! What the hell happened?"

"We are investigating. He has numerous bruises and lacerations. We have several lines of enquiry open." His phone rang. "His family has arrived. You coming?"

"No, you can deal with them. They will deal with me soon enough." I stood there shaking. I needed to be with John.

My thoughts were diverted as John's family came out of the lift. I saw his father's face, blaming me for creating havoc in their gilded boy's life. His mother looked ashen and had obviously been crying. I walked away, hoping to find the doctor while they bombarded O'Reilly with questions. Wish I had his stamina. I was surprised when Ginge came across to me.

"Are you okay, mate?"

"Just bearing up, don't know what is going on, just want to see him."

He patted my shoulder. "He's a tough boy, lucky to have you."

Just then the doctor came over, a magnet to the father with O'Reilly in hot pursuit.

"Mr Willadoro is now stable and speaking slowly. Will you come with me, Mr Burke?"

"I'm his father. I should see him."

"He is asking for Mr Burke and one person is enough at this stage."

"Nothing but trouble," yelled the father.

"Give it a rest, Dad. We need to focus on Johnno," from Ginge.

I turned and followed the doctor into the room, preparing for the worst.

Looking at John, I saw a weak, ashen-faced young man. As I took his hand, his arms bandaged, he opened his eyes and smiled, then he wept. Leaning forward, I was emotional, trying to be brave for him, but the tears came. I glanced at the doctor, who nodded his approval.

"On the mend, John, you will be okay." The doctor said he would leave us alone for a short time, but they still needed to keep monitoring him.

The door closed. We kissed. "What is happening, Robbie? I don't remember anything; did I stuff up? I didn't drink much, I kept refusing more drinks. You know I wouldn't ever hurt you."

His voice was low, and I could hear the pain and confusion in it. My throat tightened. "I know that, but what I don't know is what happened at the pub. The doctor said you were drugged, and the police suspect you were assaulted. They will tell us more soon, I hope. The policeman is a suspicious man."

John moaned. "What? What was the drug?"

"Oh, by the way, your parents, Ginge and Maureen, have arrived."

He rolled his eyes. "Bet Dad thinks it's all your fault again."

I mentioned his dad had ignored me, but Ginge had a go at him, and came over to see if I was okay.

"Good, hope Ginge can escape too."

"Robbie, how did I get here?"

"Well, remember I dropped you off at the pub?"

"Not really but go on."

"I rang you at about twelve, got voice mail and, shortly after, Todd rang on your phone and said you were on the way to hospital and the police had been called. None of it makes sense. They did tests on your blood and only found a little alcohol, but they also found some Rohypnol."

John exploded. "Fuck, not the date rape drug?"

"Calm down, John, your blood pressure."

Loud beeping, flashing lights, and the doctor and two nurses rushed in.

"Take is easy, John," said the doctor. "Hold his hand, Mr Burke."

We all sat there silently, waiting for his blood pressure to fall. Finally, the doctor said all was okay, but no more chat.

"John, I am just outside and will not leave you until I take you home, okay?" He smiled and relaxed.

As we walked out, I blurted out, "Sorry, doctor, I mentioned the Rohypnol. He got worked up."

"Understandable, Mr Burke, but I suggest for the moment, just keep to happy talk," and winked.

The flurry of doctors and nurses had caused a stir, and I was so pleased to see Ruth, who rushed up to me and hugged me, whispering, "Daddy is not a happy vegemite."

"I know, but Ginge just had a go at him." Wide-eyed, Ruth responded, "Really? There's hope yet."

CHAPTER 17

The doctor told John's family he would take them in shortly and stay with them because he was still monitoring John.

The father snidely mentioned it looked like the so-called boyfriend just caused more trouble, as usual. Fortunately, everyone ignored him.

Ruth suggested a coffee. As she walked away, I watched her walk up to John's mother, Merryl, who stood up and walked out with her. Not long after, they both walked in, talking. Merryl with her coffee sat down with Tony, and Ruth brought me my coffee. I just looked at her. She answered my look by saying, "As a mother, I know how devastating this would be for her. I think she appreciated a shoulder."

The policeman came up to us. In an official tone, he stated, "As the doctor told you, they found Rohypnol in his blood, and we are treating this as a serious matter. Charges could be laid against certain people. Mr Willadoro's friend, Todd, has contacted police and wishes to make a statement. Another young man has also contacted us. He wants to make a statement and press assault charges against three men."

"Please do not share this with anyone, as it may prejudice our case. I want to see justice done."

I was too exhausted to speak. All of this was draining me. I just wanted it to all go away, but I felt deep down this was just the tip. I asked him to join us for coffee.

We sat and drank coffee in silence. John lay nearby, exhausted, just as I felt. Ruth broke the ice by saying, in a low voice, "Detective sergeant—"

"No, please call me Pat; it will be a long night."

"Pat, these boys have been through hell. No one knows it more than me, and they deserve better. These morons who did this must be found and punished."

Pat's phone pinged; he checked it. His grim face said it all.

"What's happened?" questioned Ruth.

"You need to brace yourselves. A photo is now circulating, showing Mr Willadoro in a dishevelled state, obviously unconscious, with a man lying face down on his groin."

I buried my head in my hands and began to sob. "Will they never leave us alone?!" Ruth threw her arms around me. Then I heard him.

"You are despicable, bringing my son into disgrace." I didn't look up, as I heard our policeman bundle him away.

Soon after, Detective O'Reilly acted promptly, and arranged for the following media statement to be issued:

> *This morning at approximately 1.30 am, Mr Johnno Willadoro was admitted to hospital, unconscious. Investigations are ongoing and several witnesses have come forward and are assisting police with their inquiries.*
>
> *We are aware of a photograph being circulated showing Mr Willadoro unconscious. Considering potential police action, we caution anyone who posts this photo.*
>
> *Mr Willadoro is with his partner and family, who are distressed by this situation. The matter is being treated seriously.*

The policeman brought over a copy for us to read. It had gone live now, and he hoped it would set the record straight. He continued, "We are doing everything to complete the investigation, and I can say, off the record, your partner's friend Todd, has been very helpful. I add that he is very distressed —he may have unwillingly helped to perpetuate the incident. He has asked to see Mr Willadoro, but we have said no visitors at this stage. It will be up to you and your partner to decide that." Then he walked away to hand the copy to the family.

Sitting there with Ruth, Maureen—Ginge's wife—came over with a coffee and, sitting down, quietly spoke. "Here, you probably need another. Can I get one for you, Ruth?"

Ruth shook her head, "No.".

"You two really have been given a tough time. Not many people would keep bouncing back. Trust me, I often get told I am not good enough for Ginge. We should form our own club to rival 'First Wives Club'. Let's call it 'Not up to the Mark Club'. What'd you think?" Her smile was slightly lopsided, but I appreciated her attempt to make conversation.

"You make me laugh Maureen; you would make a good president. But you know Ginge loves you, and John loves me, so really that is all that matters. Besides, Ginge is standing up to the old boy; maybe the old boy is secretly gay and jealous."

Maureen choked and spluttered out, "God no, what a terrible ugly vision!" She kissed my cheek and walked away.

Despite Ruth's hugging me, I couldn't hold back my emotion. She patted me on the back. "Robbie, I know this is awful, but you must read between the lines. It is an obvious set-up. Sure, it went wrong and could have been a tragic accident. The police will get to the bottom of it, and if they don't, I will!"

"I hope the perpetrators have to face the police, and not you." We both laughed.

"Actually, it has also come at a very bad time, Ruth, and I know John will understand me sharing this with you. But it's our secret, okay?"

"What secret?"

"John and I have been pursuing a possible adoption. We know you all felt surrogacy was the way to go, but we have made this decision."

"Robbie now is not a good time to discuss this. You know my thoughts; we need to wait until Johnno's well again. You will make the best ever dads and me the best ever auntie, but is adoption the right way to go?"

"Ruth, it is under way, so our families need to accept our decision. It will devastate us if this puts the kibosh on it. I will ring the agency in the morning to alert them to what is happening. I am sure, if need be, Pat will help."

"Pat?"

"Yes, Pat seems to have mellowed in relation to us. He was terse at the beginning, just thought John was out for a night with the boys and having fun, but I think he has realised now it was an attack on John. So, few people really understand John. He's a very extraordinary man. So glad I came to Jimmy's party that day."

"Yes, at least you didn't throw up on him." I ignored that comment.

The doctor came over and said I could go and see John again, but then I needed to go home. He was banning all visitors until the next day when I could spend time with him.

Walking in, I could see he had improved, and we chatted. He was full of questions, so I told him about Ginge and Maureen. He laughed. "Oh, and guess what? Ruth took your mum to get a coffee, and Tony didn't say boo." John wiped his eyes.

"John, your dad does love you, but he's a bit old school. We need to understand that and go gently; one day he will come around, I'm sure of it."

"You have the biggest heart of anyone I know and am glad I have it."

"All yours, young man."

"With all this going on, I remembered the agency. What will they think?"

"Under control; texted Clare and said I would ring her this morning to let her know about some issues that had come up and that we needed to explain.

"Oh, and by the way, I blurted out to Ruth what was happening on that front. Of course, she brought up the surrogacy thing, but I explained we had chosen our path. Sorry, just been a bit stressful."

"Don't stress, I trust you with my life; I really want to marry you and have a family."

"Maybe we need to move to the Nullarbor, where no one knows us."

He laughed, and then he sighed. "You mean me. I am the cause of all this."

"No, my man, when the sexiest footballer in the world meets the oldest gay novelist in the world, tongues will wag."

"I never see you as old. I will never ever forget the first time I saw you—a sexy, confident man who had it all together. How could I make him notice me? When you asked me what my real job was, I thought, *I'm going to marry this man*."

"What! You never told me that."

John smirked. "A boy's got to have some secrets."

"Any more secrets, Mr Willadoro?"

"No, just saved that one for a special occasion and, hell, this is one. When can I go home, babe?"

The doctor walked in. "I heard that, and as soon as I feel you are out of the woods. I am sending your partner home now, no arguments. He needs rest, and so do you. No visitors until tomorrow afternoon when Mr Burke will be back to visit, and I will assess your discharge. The police want to be kept informed. I think you both need a good night's sleep. Mr Burke, is your sister taking you home?"

"Not sure, I guess so. Haven't thought about it."

O'Reilly entered and said he would take both of us home; adding that he had arranged for police protection at my home.

"What!" I exclaimed.

"The assault on your partner is serious, so until we get to the bottom of it all, we are taking no chances. We also will have police protection for Mr Willadoro in the hospital."

Now I fully realised the enormity of what was happening.

CHAPTER 18

The doctor spoke to John. "Your parents and brother want to see you. Are you up to a short visit?"

John glanced at me.

"Ruth and I will leave; it will be easier for you."

He seemed sad but nodded to me. The doctor said they would have a very limited visit and he would remain in the room. I watched John settle with relief in his eyes as I waved and left.

On the drive home, in silence, I reflected on what John had said. We had a chance meeting that unearthed a love between two people that should have been just a simple, ongoing romance. Instead, it precipitated events that caused—oh, how to describe it ... I think I was too numb to describe it. Just remembering an afternoon at the beach was comforting; just us, sitting together laughing, two lovers, not a care in the world, no one around to care about two men happy being together. But life intrudes, and we all must deal with it.

I slept alone that night, missing the man who had become so important to me—his heavy breathing, his waking through the night, touching, his caresses, things lovers share. I cried for the man I missed that night. I tried not to think of the anger of people who caused us to be apart.

Next morning, Pat rang to say that he and his offsider needed to talk to John and suggested we have our lawyer present. I could not believe that, and I wanted to know why. He said it was protocol; it was to protect John, so there could be no suggestion that the police coerced any statements. I appreciated that and rang our friend, Andy, a lawyer who was a good friend. We would meet at the hospital.

Clare texted back and acknowledged, saying we would talk soon.

That afternoon could not come sooner. I had a troubled night's sleep, but was up early making my cheese biscuits, John's favourite. Boys love their treats. My mother always said the way to a man's heart is through his stomach, but over the years, I proved that wrong. I threw millions of recipe books out because it didn't seem to work, but John never knocked back my cooking.

The police drove us to the back entrance of the hospital through a massive media presence camped outside. Hungry for the gossip morsels. As I entered his room, I saw my man rested and bright, and we had the biggest hug. I was excited to see him so alert, but he was still baffled by the police presence. I reassured him the police would fill us in.

I also explained that Andy, our lawyer, would be there. John appeared alarmed.

"Have I done something wrong?"

"No, John, not at all. Andy is here to protect us, and O'Reilly wanted everything above board."

Andy walked in, greeting John. Straight away, I saw the anxiety fade from John's face.

O'Reilly walked in with his offsider and the discussion started. Pat began with: "Mr Willadoro, what do you remember about the night at the pub?"

"Well, from memory, sorry, still a bit hazy about the night, Robbie dropped me off at the pub. We had agreed I would ring him when I was ready to be picked up and told him it would be before midnight. We had some drinks, and the guys kept telling me to try these fancy cocktails, but I said no, beer is okay. They kept insisting and said they had a special one for the best footy guy in the team. Eventually, I agreed. It was very sweet. Next thing I saw was nurses and doctors."

"You know nothing else, like lying on the floor with someone?"

He looked stunned. "What the fuck?"

"Mr Willadoro, we believe you have been drugged, assaulted, and compromised. We have a statement from Todd Gregory, your friend, who says he now realises he was used to lure you to the pub, to have you assaulted in a comprising position. When he realised this, he attempted to stop it, but he too was assaulted.

"The guys who wanted to meet you had hired a male prostitute for a boys' fun night. The prostitute was paid $1,000 to give a 'footy mate'—excuse the expression—a blow job. But when he arrived and saw you were unconscious on the floor, he refused to be part of it. He felt it was a set-up. When he refused, he was then assaulted, his clothes ripped, and he was held down on top of you. After the photo was taken, the money was extracted from him, and he was thrown out. He complained to management that he had been assaulted, so they called their security, police, and ambulance.

"What about the photo?" asked John.

Silence.

"Robbie, have you seen it?"

"No, I haven't."

John exploded. "Do we need to? Is it fucking filth? I guess it is! They are determined to take me down. What more can they do to us, Robbie? Can't they leave us alone?! I've never ever hurt anyone; why such vindictiveness!"

"No, John, you haven't hurt anyone. In taking charge of your life, you have upset those who either cannot do that, or have a prejudice against lifestyle choices. You have taken charge of your life, and no one can take that away from you."

"Robbie, please take me home. I only feel safe with you."

You know that expression ... 'not a dry eye in the house'.

Pat stated that the young male prostitute had wanted to make a statement and press charges. He had no idea who you were, but he could see you were unconscious, and he did not want any part of it. With both statements, we have enough to lay charges. They will get top lawyers, but the weight of evidence is strong.

"Will I have to give evidence?"

"I don't know, but your lawyer will probably sort something out, so you don't."

Andy threw John a confident nod.

The doctor agreed to discharge John, and we left to go home. All John wanted to do was curl up in bed with me and we held each other in silence. No words could express the anguish we felt. Tomorrow was a new day, with a brighter future.

❍

Over the coming weeks, the dreadful scenario played out. There were police charges against three men, public outcry, and football dismissals. That is all that needed to be recorded. We were moving on. Life was ahead of us.

Todd called to see John, and I left them alone. After some time, Todd asked me to join them. His apology to John was to encompass me. He deeply regretted creating the situation that allowed what transpired.

He told us that we were his mentors as he wanted to come out as gay himself. We were the first he had told, and his family was to be next. Jokingly, he asked for pointers because he was concerned how they would react. He hoped he could find a person to make him as happy as we were.

John was so pleased. He needed to know that by standing up for himself, he had enabled others to achieve what we had.

CHAPTER 19

Soon after John's assault and, out of the blue, Clare rang me to arrange a meeting. I was so excited. "Do you have someone?"

"Can you both come and see me tomorrow at, say, 9 am?"

"I will check with John, but I'm sure it will be okay. We have been on tenterhooks."

John agreed, and that night over drinks, we speculated. I felt sure there must be someone; why else call us in? All the discussing had been done. Neither of us slept much that night.

With some trepidation, we walked into Clare's office and were comforted by her welcome.

"Sit down guys, I need to have a discussion with you. I will lay it all out, then we can talk.

"We have twin boys aged eight who are to be adopted out. They are Vietnamese and their parents were killed in a car accident about two years ago. Since then, they have been cared for by their grandfather. They are all Australian citizens, but the grandfather is getting old and needs to go into care.

"Our assessment team all agree that because of their age, ethnicity, the sudden loss of parents and now their grandfather, the children need a couple who could best deal with their sensitive situation. The team felt that, from your documented profile, you would be great parents for them.

Your dealings with adversity and your cultural awareness make you ideal.

"Having met you both, I endorsed it and expanded my thoughts about you both.

"The grandfather has asked that he meet any potential parents before a decision is made, and we have agreed. Once the grandfather approves, you will meet the boys. They will have limited input because of their age; however, we would gauge their interactions with you. I will give you time to consider."

We looked at each other, our eyes welling up before John appealed, "Any chance we can see a photo of the boys?"

Clare instantly handed us a photo. "I knew you would want to see them; I could witness your positive reaction."

Taking the photo, we saw the two cutest boys with beaming smiles. We hugged each other while looking at their photo. Clare had discreetly left the room.

"John, they have your smile." Looking at our boys, we knew it would happen.

Clare returned after a while and asked how we felt about the idea of Vietnamese twins. We told her we wanted to meet the grandfather and hoped we passed the test.

"So pleased to hear that. They will be very fortunate boys." She explained that the grandfather would be fully briefed about us and our relationship.

So, it was time to wait. Hopefully, the tide was turning.

Some days later, Clare called to say the grandfather was confused about two men living together as a couple. She had several meetings with him and the interpreter, who was always there in the discussions. She would come back to us when resolved, one way or the other.

Our hearts sank.

Finally, Clare called to say the appointment to meet the grandfather was to be arranged, however the grandfather still had doubts.

We asked her how we should prepare. She said, "Just be yourselves, just how you were with me. I'm sure you won't have a worry."

Arriving at the grandfather's house, we met Clare and Toy, the interpreter, a young Vietnamese man. Clare explained that Ong Noi—the grandfather—spoke some English, but the adoption agency needed to make sure he fully understood everything that was said. He opened the door and welcomed us in, where everyone was introduced. He beckoned us to the dining table set up for morning tea. The teapot was on a low burner, accompanied by simple biscuits on a plate. He poured us all a cup; we thanked him, then all drank our tea.

He asked us to tell him where we lived, how we met, our future plans for the boys.

Toy suggested we answer the questions, and he would stop us when he needed to translate, or if Ong Noi indicated he needed help. Toy explained the two of them had discussed same-sex relationships, which were foreign to him. He now felt Ong Noi had a better understanding of it, but was still wary. This was his first experience of it.

John gave a run down about our home, showing him photos and the boys' bedroom. Ong Noi scrutinised the photos, showing great interest.

John continued about our life, leaving all the ugly bits out as Clare said that was not necessary; Ong Noi had been fully briefed about us.

When it was my turn to speak, Ong Noi put his hand up. I stopped. He spoke to Toy, who translated to us, "I understand you both had difficulties in the early days, but you worked together, and you did well. Couples should always work together, good. However, my grandsons are my primary concern. Despite having your relationship explained, I need to be sure, as I always considered they would go to a couple like my daughter and son-in-law. I hope you both understand."

We nodded our agreement.

I wasn't sure I could go on. Such a caring man. He handed me a handkerchief to wipe my eyes when he saw I had become emotional. I slowly continued explaining about our plans for educating the boys while John handed him photos of the proposed school. I told him that it was our desire to keep the boys in contact with their Vietnamese heritage. Also, we would want the boys to keep in close contact with him and put it to him that we would all meet every Sunday for a picnic lunch. Then I passed the handkerchief back to him as he cried.

Time passed with lots of chat, laughter, and a few tears. It must have been a difficult time for him to realise how life was changing for him.

We left with hope in our hearts.

After several sleepless nights, Clare called. "It's all go boys! You meet the boys next Sunday. Ong Noi has not said a definite yes, however, he wants to meet you with the boys."

We were overjoyed that it had gone a step further. Not all was lost yet. Hell, another week! We kept ourselves busy, but the looming adoption was always at the back of our minds and the very real possibility it would not happen. At the back of our minds, we knew not everyone accepted our same-sex relationship. It was foreign to many.

I told John I was scared; he asked why. I explained it was a big thing to take on, and it had only now really hit home. Concerned, he asked if I wanted to stop it now. I hugged him, shaking my head. "No! Just hold me and say it will be alright."

He looked at me, beaming. "Robbie, if you can handle me, you can handle anything. Trust me, the boys will be easy," and we both laughed.

"Yes, young man, you can be a handful, and I know we can do it together."

Sunday came. I hadn't been so nervous as this since I told my parents I was gay! John laughed and told me I was lucky; he was still trying to explain his sexuality to his.

"I intend to win over Daddy Tony, no matter what."

"Good luck, Uncle Robbie."

We arrived at Ong Noi's house with Clare and Toy. The twins anxiously checked us out, as we did them. It was two nervous boys meeting two nervous boys. We were introduced to Huy and Liem.

John broke the ice with, "Boys, I have a ball here. Feel like a kick and a play?"

They jumped up and ran to him; in seconds, they were in the garden. Need I say that John is a natural dad.

We all watched while Ong Noi looked on with warmth and a few tears.

Clare said, "I knew from the moment I met you guys it would happen one day."

The afternoon rolled on. There was chat with the boys about living with us and how they felt. We explained to them we were two dads, and it was different from their mum and dad.

We asked how they felt about that. They exchanged glances and grinned, saying, "It's funny."

We could sense the trust developing between us. It was difficult for boys so young. We discussed our proposals to see Ong Noi each week, promising to take them to Vietnam to connect with their family members they had never met. They were young, but we felt they liked that idea.

The boys came up to me and asked if I would play ball with them too? "Yes," I said, "but you need to teach me."

Lots of laughter as John, I, and the boys kicked and passed the ball around. The boys screamed with laughter at me because I got it wrong most of the time by falling over.

By the end of the day, I sorta guessed we may have a family, which gave me a paternal feeling for the first time. I knew John was excited that this would enrich our relationship.

So, we waited, waited, and waited ...

At least, it felt like a long time, but it was only two days later when Clare called us and said the boys wanted to come and live with us. Ong Noi had given his blessing and was so pleased to still be part of our family. Wow was that icing on the *banh duc*!

CHAPTER 20

We were on a high with the impending arrival of the boys when Todd rang; he wanted to drop in on us. I hadn't seen much of him, although he kept in touch with John; they had been working together in the real estate business.

Todd had retired from footy after feeling so let down by some teammates who had used him to create the incident with John.

John invited him over on Sunday afternoon for a barbie. He arrived and seemed a bit nervous but sat down with a drink. Then totally unexpectedly, he blurted out we had given him so much courage to come out as gay, that at long last, he had met someone who was becoming part of his life.

"Wow," stated John. "We want to meet him."

"Actually, he is in the car outside ... I wanted to surprise you."

We were taken aback, but asked Todd to bring him in. Nothing prepared us to see him bring in Detective Sergeant O'Reilly.

John exclaimed, "What?", as we exchanged pleasantries.

Todd explained. "Pat rang me to tell me the investigation was over, so he didn't need to contact me again. I must admit I felt a bit sad; he had treated me so well and I liked him. Next day, however, he rang and said, 'Pat here, feel like coffee some time?' He explained he was off the case, so he was free to do a social catch up. The rest, as they say, is history."

Pat professed that during his interviews with Todd he found he had warmed to him, but it would have been unprofessional to do anything about it. He could not wait for the case to be wrapped up until, "I 'grabbed the bull by the horns', as they say."

"I am sorry you guys went through a lot of trauma but, if it helps, a new romance blossomed out of it. We have much to thank you for."

John looked at me, winked, and said, "Bubbles all round!" It was a great night.

CHAPTER 21

I don't think John and I had ever been so nervous as when we drove to collect the boys. Clare was there to ensure a smooth changeover. When we greeted Liem and Huy, we hugged them. We wanted to go cautiously as they were young and basically going to live with strangers.

John suggested he drive, and that I sit in the back with the boys and talk as we drove home. I told them we would be taking them to their new school on Monday.

John had taken to being a dad with all the enthusiasm and determination that had made him the great footy player he had been. He had done incredible research and found there was a small private school, fortunately near us, that had a high percentage of Asian and other ethnic students. We felt this was important for the boys and we had been to see the principal several times to talk through all the potential issues. Our biggest concern was being a same-sex couple and how that might impact. The principal, Rowena, was a woman in her fifties; she was forthright, very no-nonsense, and assured us it was not an issue. She revealed that the school had several children with same-sex parents, both male and female, some themselves being Asian.

It was, to say the least, and I guess not unexpected, that the drive home was not a ride in the park. There were awkward conversations between strangers, but there were good feelings. Arriving home, we took the boys on a tour of the house, showing them their bedroom because we had decided they should share, at least for a while, until they settled in.

They were excited about the pool and asked if they were allowed to use it.

The four of us sat down and we explained to the boys that this was their home too, and they must feel free to relax in it and enjoy it. We suggested some ground rules, but explained all four of us would observe those, too.

"Just ask if it's pool time," we explained. "There will be play time, study time, and house time, like making beds. We all want to work as a team and want you to be happy here."

They were excited and kept grinning at each other. I couldn't help but think, *This is going to work.*

John then asked, "Remember when we discussed living with us? We wondered what you would like to call us. We made a few suggestions, and we wondered what you had both decided?"

They checked with each other and giggled. Huy asked, "Can we decide?"

"Of course, guys," I said. "You must be happy with what you call us, and it will mean a lot to us, if both of you decide. We are a family now."

"We think," taking John's hand, "it should be Dad," and taking mine, "Bo." It was time for a group hug, which lasted for ages. I knew then that it was truly going to be okay.

I made a simple dinner—chicken and salad with some ice cream to finish. The plates were empty. After a bit of TV, we decided bedtime. We tucked the boys in and told them if they were worried or needed anything, we were just in the next room. A kiss goodnight and lights out.

John and I retired and had the light on for a bit of reading. We felt our door should be left open, so if they did get up, they felt secure. Start how we need to move on; we both agreed.

About fifteen minutes later, we saw two little faces peering around the door frame. John called out, "Come in guys, what's the matter?"

"We feel a bit lonely."

"Okay, come; jump in," which they did with much enthusiasm. So, our first night was amazing. They curled up between us and were sound asleep in minutes, just some gentle snoring, which they shared with their louder dad. No escape for me.

The next day, we stayed at home. In the pool, John played ball with them, so it was a happy family day. I was kept busy making sure my boys were well fed. I had never felt so happy and contented. That night they cheerfully remained in their own beds, having overcome the fear of being in a new place.

Monday morning, all four of us arrived at school. The boys met the principal, who took them off to the classrooms, with the boys giving us a big wave.

I must admit we had an anxious day wondering how it would all go. We were early to collect them and watched as they came out merrily chatting and laughing with their classmates. It wasn't till they got to the footpath they looked for us. John and I were so relieved as it appeared as if they had settled right in.

Our two boys rushed up to us yelling, "Dad, Bo, Dad, Bo," at the top of their voices.

The ride home was laid back and happy. They didn't stop talking about what they had done, who their new friends were, and the great Vietnamese style lunch I had packed.

Arriving home, John and I sank into chairs exhausted by the day but so happy it had gone well. It was time for a drink while the boys had fun in the pool. John beamed at me. "Robbie, we have our family."

I loved watching John playing with the boys, in the pool, with a football, and games they made up. I joined in, at times, which caused the boys' much laughter. However, it was great to give the three of them time together. It recharged John's batteries.

CHAPTER 22

We had told the boy's grandfather that we wanted him to be part of our family, so we suggested each Sunday we go to visit with him at the aged care home and have a picnic lunch. John found a lovely park next door, and we soon found a table which would become our favourite spot. John and I discussed the idea that I prepare some Vietnamese food which both Ong Noi and the boys would love, adding that it would expand John's culinary tastes. I got a half smile. He had been brought up with a lot of Italian dishes, plus steak and veg, but I wanted him to explore and excite his taste buds. He agreed, although he still didn't want to lose that T-bone.

On our first Sunday, there was a lot of laughter as the boys hugged Ong Noi. The park was a good idea as it enabled John and the boys to play ball, cricket, and all those other games that boys love to do. Further, it entertained Ong Noi no end. As I started to unpack the lunch, I saw his eyes light up. I am sure he thought he was in for a pie and salad. He stared at the food and commented as I brought it out.

"Oh, *banh mi*, yes, my favourite *nem nuong*." I decided not to attempt too many dishes that first time. "So much food," he said.

"Well, Ong Noi, we will just have to pack up what is left, and you can finish it up for dinner and for tomorrow. I will put it in the kitchen fridge for you." His beaming smile was gratitude enough.

I had taken the liberty of calling the manager to see if leftovers could be put in the community kitchen fridge for him. I explained to him about the Vietnamese food, and he agreed they would make a special allowance for him because they couldn't accommodate ethnic food needs like that with daily meals.

The Vietnamese picnic sandwich (*banh mi*) was easy to prepare ahead of time, and I needed to do this with the grilled pork rolls (*nem nuong*) for ease of transport. I wrapped the grilled pork rolls in lettuce, cucumber, and mint and finally in the rice paper, so it was ready for us to dip in the bean sauce. We had not told the boys what was being served, so when I called them over there was much excitement and more hugging of Ong Noi. Even John shook his head. "Any more surprises for me, old man?"

"Relax, young man. I always keep a couple up my sleeve." I got the smile.

"Well, boys, let's eat."

I must say, as they tucked in so much, I worried Ong Noi might not have any leftovers for supper. Over lunch, we talked about the boy's school routine. They told their grandfather what they had been doing, and each had prepared a drawing for him, which really delighted him. As the meal finished, he looked at us both. He had a grin on his face and, with a nod he said, "Thank you."

With deep sincerity, John replied, "Thank you for entrusting the boys into our care."

He nodded in appreciation. I then asked him if he had any tips for me to improve my dishes. He looked at me, puzzled, but I assured him I wanted to learn more about his culture and food.

He chuckled. "Add little minced anchovy. It always helps, so good for you."

John and I exchanged a glance because he hates anchovies, especially on his pizza.

So, to dessert, and I confessed we called at the local Vietnamese bakery to pick up *pandan banh bo nuong*—a Vietnamese honeycomb cake. I am still learning, but it went down well. I asked Ong Noi to suggest some dishes to me and he said he would write some down for me. Ong Noi was sad to see us go, but brightened up when we said we would be back again next Sunday.

So back to those recipe books!

CHAPTER 23

A week after the boys' arrival, we invited both families over for a barbie. It was ostensibly for John's birthday, but the family and close friends knew it was the wedding. We had drawn a mud map to show the boys where everyone slotted in, and they seemed excited to meet and have extended family.

The families all arrived at the same time. Unfortunately, John's dad, his mother, and Tony Junior did not come even though they knew of the wedding. Ginge and his wife, Maureen, did, though. I walked with them out onto the veranda, and they all saw John playing ball with the boys. They observed the joy on John's face—a proud dad.

On seeing everyone, John called out, "Come on boys, let's meet the family."

Taking their hands, they walked up the stairs; the boys were the centre of attention.

No announcement of the wedding had been made but on the day of the birthday barbie for John, there were rumours circulating about an intended wedding. We issued no statements and ignored the gossip. That day, a media circus had erupted, and our street was lined with press, TV vans, and the like. It made John anxious, so I sent him into the back garden to play with the boys. He was always the happiest being with them.

That morning, we had told the boys about the wedding. We kept it quiet as you cannot rely on youngsters to keep a secret. We had become used to them running into our room in the morning and bouncing on the bed; they didn't seem at all concerned both dads were in the same bed. It always was a great catch-up time for the four of us. We had built a team.

We told them that we would be getting married that day and they would be part of the ceremony because we were a family. We were their parents, and we wanted to be married. The excitement in their eyes was wonderful. We weren't sure if they fully understood, but they knew there was a party involved.

They wanted to know what to wear. John told them, "Whatever you like." They exclaimed it had to be really special and rushed off to decide. We wondered what they would choose. I must admit, we were not expecting the outfits they chose. Huy had his Spiderman outfit on and Liem his Wonder Woman outfit. It made a change from the usual formal wedding attendant's attire.

The costumes had been previously acquired for a fancy dress party. When Liem had chosen Wonder Woman, I asked him why. He said he loved the colours. Children are so innocent, and we accepted it. I told John his dad would love it if he saw them. John fell about laughing.

John said that our wedding day was not a day for me to be in the kitchen, so we arranged some caterers and a barman who turned up early to set up. The house was alive with activity, and we were lucky to have Ruth running around barking orders. We kept out of her way. We had to admit she did a great job though, and had Barry and Jimmy running around with flowers, tablecloths, even balloons, although we had said to keep it simple. Ruth remarked with a smirk, "No jumping castle?" I ignored her, but John cracked up.

We had insisted on no wedding presents, and everyone agreed. However, a dear friend, an artist, was adamant he wanted to give us something to mark our new beginning with the boys. It was one of his paintings which he said, 'This symbolises the love you have for each other and a new beginning." It has remained a treasure throughout our lives.

Family and our few guests started arriving amongst a hail of flashlights together with our friend Trish, our marriage celebrant. We received a few comments when the boys were seen in their striking outfits. The time arrived, and we all assembled on the veranda. John and I stood together with the boys on either side of us, outshining us in their colourful outfits. I could see John was nervous and asked him if he was okay.

"Robbie, from the day I met you, I dreamed of this day. I worried it wouldn't happen, but now, here it is. Wow! So happy to make you happy."

"We are really together now, forever." I squeezed his hand.

However, I knew John was sad that his parents and family were not coming. It highlighted to John that he hadn't been able to proudly introduce his sons to them.

We put our arms around the boys as the ceremony progressed. Trish told the gathering we had exchanged our vows with each other privately, so our commitment to each other was total. Finally, we were a married couple with children. Surrounded by family and friends, the four of us hugged and kissed.

The party rolled on and everyone was on a high. The boys loved being the centre of attention, although I noticed they didn't move far from the food table.

After the ceremony and all the hugs and kisses, I told John I had an idea. "Let's call the media's bluff. Let's open the gate, go outside, you announce, 'We are now married, please take your photos,' then we can all go home."

John was not sure, but trusting me, he agreed.

The gate opened, and we walked out to a startled media crowd. They had expected to be ignored. There was silence.

Then the street was a blaze with lights, fortunately no trees caught fire! Multiple microphones were shoved in our faces, followed by a barrage of questions. We stood there silently. John waited for the frenzy to subside and said, "I am happy to tell you my partner, Robbie, and I married this afternoon. We hope that now we can get on with our lives quietly, with our boys. Thank you all." Then adding, with that smile, "If you have all your photos, you can all go home now; take the rest of the day off."

We waved and as we turned, the sound of loud applause from up and down the street stopped us in our tracks. We gave a final wave, then walked inside, closed the gate and hugged as two special people in our lives raced up to join the hug.

The next day, for the first time, the media gave us what they call good press. We had been relegated to that wonderfully comfortable zone called suburbia—'married with kids'. They now had other fish to fry.

CHAPTER 24

About a year after the boys arrived, we planned our first visit to Vietnam. The boys were excited when we talked about it, knowing they would meet family members unknown to them. Through Ong Noi, and with the help of the boys, we contacted a cousin of the boys' father—Thanh. He lived in a remote area in the north, in a small village called Pac Ngoi, just over two hundred kilometres north of Hanoi.

The boys were right onto Google and told us Pac Ngoi Village is in the Nam Mau commune, of the Ba Be District, and is famous for its stilt houses of the Tay people. It is located on the banks of Leng River close to Ba Be Lake. "All villagers are Tay people," the boys announced with admiration, as they claimed they too must be Tay people, but proudly added, "You are still our dads."

It was a whole new world for them, one which we embraced with them. We arranged our visit to coincide with the boys' school holidays. Luckily, it was also school holidays in Vietnam so they could have time with their young relations. The boys discovered that a lot of the stilt houses had become homestays for tourists, so we contacted Thanh. Remarkably, his house was a homestay.

We asked if we could book, but he insisted we would be his guests. We politely said we wanted to pay the normal rate so, after a lot of emails, we settled on a ten percent discount. That way, we all felt comfortable.

In discussing it all with the boys, we decided we would visit the local market each day and bring back fruit and vegetables for the household. That excited the boys. However, I had a sneaking suspicion John would smuggle some T-bones in his luggage. I thought a final inspection before we left would be in order.

As the departure time approached, we could see the boys were nervous. It would bring back so many memories surrounding their parents, so we spent a lot of time talking them through the visit and their need to discuss any concerns with us. They assured us they really wanted to go and collected a strange variety of 'Australiana' to take with them. We gave no guidance, as it was to be their choice. But we did have a chuckle.

The day arrived. All the checking in and airport departure formalities were done and, of course, as usual, even with sunnies, we were the centre of attention—the boys adding to that. We flew business class, which shielded us somewhat. Of course, the boys charmed the cabin crew and at times we had to gently stop the continuous flow of nibbles and drinks they ordered.

We flew into Hanoi and had two nights there to rest up and give the boys their first taste of the country before we invaded the relatives. Being surrounded by so many people of their heritage, the boys were intrigued. Yes, it was a very new experience for them. Their language skills were perfect, so meal ordering was heaven. John didn't even mention the T-bone word. Time had adjusted him to Asian cuisine ... somewhat.

We travelled up to Pac Ngoi Village by various local buses, which could only be described as an adventure. John had been exposed to road travel in Bali, but this was something else. He remained quiet. The boys were so excited it was hard to keep them seated. The various comfort stops gave us a break while a beer kept John refreshed. Having travelled through Bac Kan, we arrived at Pac Ngoi to be greeted by a very excited group of 'rellies', led by Thanh.

The boys were quiet; they were suddenly overwhelmed by it all and gripped our hands. As the younger rellies surrounded them, chatting away, any anxiety experienced by the twins dissipated. Soon, they were back to their animated selves.

We walked through the village in awe of the wonderful stilt houses. We did a lot of smiling, nodding, and sharing the few polite words we knew, "*Xin chào, khỏe không?*". We pointed to ourselves with: "*Tên tôi là* Johnno and *tên tôi là* Robbie". I laughed at John, "We are dorks," which set him right off.

We arrived at Thanh's homestay stilt house. It was a traditional construction built of timber with palm and straw leaves for the roof on stilts above the ground. When we arrived, we followed the custom by removing our shoes before climbing the ladder into the house. Having stayed in a longhouse in Borneo a long time ago, I knew what to expect, but my three boys were wide-eyed. I winked at John, but he seemed lost. We sat on the floor and were served tea. There was lots of chat, mainly from the boys, John and I having exhausted our local vocabulary on the walk to the house.

John saved the day by producing a ball. He suggested he take the boys outside to join all the other kids for a kick and toss around. This was followed by the usual yelling and laughter, and I was glad to see my man lively and happy again. I knew he had been anxious about how it would all go, so it was a relief to see him frolicking with the kids. Also, it really was a joy to see our sons so happy, playing with and enjoying their local families. I was with the oldies, so I did my best. We were lucky Thanh's younger brother, who was an English teacher, was home on holidays. He became our translator and enjoyed getting his head around our Aussie language.

That night we shared a dinner with our family hosts and other guests. The local food was delicious, which my man enjoyed. But I guessed a T-bone would be defrosted as soon as we returned home. Thanh offered us a local beer; surprisingly, I actually enjoyed it. However, John's gracious comments let me know it certainly wasn't John's favourite Aussie beer!

As we retired, Thanh explained that sleeping arrangements were long rows of mats and blankets—side by side. I felt John's discomforted look behind me, but not for long.

Thanh explained they had set up our bedding in a separate room for our privacy. We withdrew to our room with a relieved John, though the boys loved the idea of communal sleeping with their new family members. As we cuddled up together on futon-like mattresses, I quietly reminded John the walls were paper thin. He laughed, whispering, "I can be quiet, just hope the stilts hold up." I made no comment or complaint.

The week went well with local walks and tourist visits; we even bumped into fellow Aussie tourists, some of whom were startled to see their footy hero there. Fortunately, they left us in peace. We were a formidable walking group and very noisy. John was in his element. We were both popular with the very young ones wanting to hold our hands as we wandered around the sights. John was busy with his camera, so it would be a long video when the holiday was over.

Our departure day was sad. The boys were downhearted, and even John and I were emotional. Everyone had accepted the four of us as family, but the sadness was lightened when we said we would be back each year. As we departed on the bus, the boys waved till everyone was out of sight and then they curled up beside us and we hugged them. The rocking of the bus lulled them into sleep. Gazing with contentment as two little boys slept and snored, I mouthed to John, "Take after you." I got a look. Was he saving the smile?

Each year we returned, and as the boys grew, it became more a part of their lives. Deep friendships developed. Thanks to the internet and modern communication systems, it was so much easier for them to always keep in touch. We were sure Ong Noi would be happy.

CHAPTER 25

Enjoying our drinks in the garden as the boys played enthusiastically in the pool, John received a call from his dad late one Sunday afternoon. Looking at me as he answered, putting his finger to his lips, he turned on the speaker.

"Hi Dad, how's it going?"

"Okay, Johnno, and you?"

"All good, Dad, so what's up?"

"You know your mother's having a big birthday next month. I asked her what she wanted, and she told me. She reminded me I never refuse her anything, which is true, but she's dropped me right in it with this one."

"Why, Dad, are the diamonds too expensive?"

"Don't fuck with me. That would be easy."

"Dad, spit it out. You can afford anything."

"This won't cost me a penny."

"Wow, sounds good to me. Tell me."

"Your bloke about?"

"Just spit it out."

"Okay. She wants a party, and she said I must ask you and, and your bloke to have it at your place with all the family, and the guests she invites. Dropped me right in it."

"Dad, would that be too hard a thing to do?

"Fucking hard for me, nothing against you, but ..."

'We would love it, Dad. I am so pleased you rang. We both understand. It will be okay."

"Easy for you to say. Well, shit happens as you get older. You need to accept things or are made too. Just have crates of my favourite beer in. Geez, I'm gonna need it. And to top it off, she wants to be invited over soon to discuss the food and all that with, um, um ..."

"He has a name, Dad, Robbie."

"Give me time, Johnno."

"Tell Mum to ring and we will arrange."

John hung up. I looked at him wide-mouthed, "Wow, your mother's got spirit. Do you think she and Ruth have been conniving?"

John cracked up.

About a week later, Merryl turned up. We were strangers. John was out because Merryl had announced it was just to be the two of us. Was I nervous? HELL, YES!

I held out my hand when she arrived, but she pushed it aside and hugged me. Unable to contain my delight, I blabbered, "Well, Merryl, I have to say I admire you very much."

A wicked smirk engulfed her face. "You should, I'm your mother-in-law. So, let's plan a party, Robbie."

Asking her if she would like tea or coffee, she laughed, "I thought you boys kept bubbles in the house?"

So, with bubbles in hand, Merryl looked at me. "You are my son's partner, or should I say husband? Anyway, I know nothing about you other than the little that Johnno has told us. I want to change that. My husband is a wonderful husband and father, caring but stubborn.

"Johnno's lifestyle choice came out of the blue and knocked Tony for six. He had no idea how to handle it. He had no concept of anyone who was gay, however with gentle handling, Tony will come around. People think I am a mouse, but I can roar when needed.

"As Johnno grew up, I always wondered about him. He's a sensitive boy, but I knew he had his father's determination. I reckoned that one day he would work it out. Everyone needs to find that special one. Over coffee, the way he talked, I knew he had. Oh, (holding up her glass) the tide's gone out."

I cautiously topped up her glass, which she held out until the tide was right in!

We talked for hours. I had seen the strength John got from his dad, and now all the sensitivity and love from his mum. I hardly noticed we had moved onto the second bottle. What was that about planning a party menu?

John walked in. What a sight, both of us laughing away, well into bubbles.

"What the ...? What are you two up to?"

Merryl managed to get out, "Showing Robbie how to live."

"Are you two pissed? The boys will be home soon. Mum, I better take you home, maybe some coffee first."

Wow! What an afternoon!

The day of the party arrived, and John was on edge. I was, well, not sure how to describe it, apprehensive I think does it.

Merryl had insisted that Ruth and her family be there. Last time they all saw each other was at the hospital. I noticed Ruth and Merryl at the bubbles table; they had all the appearances of being besties. *Hello, what's going on?*

Tony was looking anxious, so John took the boys up to meet him, explaining this was his dad. John had briefed the boys, so Huy looked at him. "Shall we call you Tony or Poppy Tony?"

Tony seemed lost for words.

Huy continued, "Dad told us you trained him, and his success was because of you. My brother and I play soccer at school, so maybe you can help us with our soccer?"

Tony looked at them, then at John. Liem handed Tony their soccer ball, and they each took a hand, leading him down into the garden.

Tony had his back to us, but he had an audience glued to see the reaction. The boys started kicking the ball around. Tony just stood there watching as we did. Tony then started talking to them and before long was barking orders, which didn't faze the boys. They were screaming with delight.

John looked at me, beaming. No room for a smile. I nodded my head to the left, and we watched the new besties laughing at the bar. *Hmmm, gonna be an interesting afternoon.*

All the noise and shouting from the garden made it obvious that it was now 'Poppy Tony'.

Encircling his arm around my waist, John clinked my glass. "Today has been a long time coming."

John took my glass as Ruth sidled up to me. "Looks like we have happy families at last."

"Yes," I replied. "I wonder if the besties had a finger in the pie?"

Ruth looked me straight in the eye. "What happens at the hairdressers stays at the hairdressers." She walked off.

Merryl came up to me. "Not drinking?"

"John is topping me up. You have done well, mother-in-law."

"Don't call me that, so formal, and I love your sister. Such fun."

"She has her moments. So ... had a few too many perms lately, Merryl?" She smiled.

"You have children now. They will be the centre of your life, believe me. The best present I received today was seeing Tony so happy. I knew he needed his family back and grandchildren were the bonus." She walked off, waving her empty glass.

Tony walked onto the veranda and headed straight for me. I braced myself, wondering what to expect.

"I wanted my son to be the top footballer which he achieved; just didn't expect him to retire so early. I move in a lot of business circles and people say to me: 'Your son is one of the most respected real estate agents in Brisbane. You must be proud.' I am. He made some good choices. You done well for my son. Keep it up. Just don't get my wife pissed again."

He laughed and walked off.

John handed me a glass. "You are the popular one. What did Dad say?

I recounted.

He laughed. "I cannot believe my dad today; the boys love him, and he won't leave them alone. How did this happen?"

Cryptically, I replied, "You'd be surprised what a good perm can do." He shook his head in bewilderment.

"Well, the boys are going to be exhausted tonight. Mum keeps telling me about all the outings she plans for them. Watch when they leave; the boys could be kidnapped."

"John, I am so pleased for you. You deserve it."

"No, we deserve it. After they all leave, and the boys go to bed, let's celebrate."

"What more bubbles?"

"Who said anything about bubbles? No sleep for you tonight, old man."

CHAPTER 26

As time went by, it was fascinating to watch the personalities of our young boys develop. Above all, they acted as a team.

Huy had a strong personality, saw things black and white, but took time to think through the final decisions he had to make.

Liem was softer, with a gentle temperament and accepted everything at face value. Huy acted like a big brother and ensured no one took advantage of Liem.

Although the school seemed to lack bullies, no one would attempt to bully Liem. The brothers played jokes on each other, wrestled, and did all those things boys do, but never to the point of hurting one another.

Their love for us grew and I could see Huy was a great observer; he knew how to get around me from just watching and copying his dad. But he always respected me when I put my foot down. I also got that smile. What a smile! Torture doubled.

We knew it would happen one day. The boys asked if they could have a puppy. All their friends had one, so we agreed to talk about it.

I was happy about it and John agreed. But he was concerned that with me working from home, it was just another thing for me to deal with. Despite a cleaning lady coming in each week, I already did all the cooking and various household chores. Further, I took the boys to and from school, as well as soccer practice, matches and all the other school events that cropped up when John couldn't make it. He knew it impacted on my work and was aware of my need to be an equal contributor financially.

John did what he could, but his real estate business had kicked off well. He always arranged things so he could be there for the boys' soccer matches as often as he could. It helped that the boys were in the same team. We had long discussions about this. However, John was adamant that what I did gave him and the boys a home life other people often dream about.

"We went into this together. Contributions take many forms, and I feel you do more than I could ever hope to contribute. It's not always about money." He was a hard man to argue with and closed the discussion with that smile.

So we were back to the puppy talk. I had seen an article in the local paper for people to be puppy carers until they are ready to be trained as seeing-eye dogs. I felt sure there would be a great attachment to the puppy, so it would be hard on them to see the puppy leave.

John looked at me with the comment, "Maybe not a good option."

"Let's sleep on it. I always find that works."

"Beautiful man, your sleeps always come up with a solution. What is it about your sleeps?"

"Provided, however, I am not interrupted by a randy young footballer!"

He put his arms around me, kissed me, and sometime later—much later—we fell asleep.

I awoke to find my man propped up and smiling at me.

"What?"

"Robbie, I am waiting for your solution."

"Well, I wondered if we explained to the boys that they came into our lives for us to care for them, until they go out into the world with careers. Then it was just like that."

"Lover, gotta hand it to you."

So we talked to the boys as they understood about giving back to the community, which we had involved them with.

John and I were very keen for the boys to retain their Vietnamese heritage, so we had involved their grandfather in helping to teach the boys some Vietnamese folk songs. I was not very musical but took the boys to guitar lessons so they could accompany themselves and sing some songs.

We started going to some aged care homes on Sunday afternoons to do some short performances. The boys loved that and subsequently, the parents of their friends asked if their children could join in. The children at the school came from a multitude of cultural backgrounds.

We agreed after getting the parents together and explaining we were a same-sex couple. We were surprised by the reaction. Some were happy, and others raised the blue card issue. Some walked out, some stayed. We offered to get the card to make it work. So, the singing group continued and grew. Our trips to Vietnam helped us film singers to get the accents correct. I think we peaked in the first year—much to our delight—as the group was asked to sing at each school graduation night after that.

Now, back to the puppies. We asked the boys what they thought; it had to be their decision. They both looked at each other and Liem said, "I can live with that." Huy came back with, "Me too, I can live with that." I think I have heard that before. Decision made.

When Toby, the most beautiful puppy arrived, John and our boys were elated. Poor Toby would be loved to death.

We had been given all the instructions for his daily routine and how to care for him. The boys made up long lists of their chores for Toby—washing, feeding, walking—but they adored him and never needed to be prompted to care for him.

However, walking was a challenge because of the age of the boys; we didn't like them walking alone. We were fortunate in that we lived not too far from the school, so I would walk the boys and Toby to school in the morning. Afterwards, Toby would accompany me to a local coffee haunt—popular with all the other dog lovers—for a flat white, before returning home for work, as you do.

Over the coming years, we fostered several puppies, and the boys always looked forward to welcoming a new one into our family.

I had never had a dog before, though Ruth and I had several when we were growing up, but I enjoyed having Toby and his fellow dogs around. Now in my late fifties, I could not believe the happiness I enjoyed with a partner and all the benefits he brought with our own family and a puppy, to boot. Looking back to those dark times of my youth, life was more settled now and especially with the fact John's father had finally accepted us and made himself the boys' coach.

The boys played soccer at school on weekends and, at times, Tony took them to the matches. He was now a super proud grandfather, while Uncle Ginge was right behind him. Huy and Liem loved Poppy Tony, and I have to confess. I realised Tony had the same love in his heart as John, but found it hard to express. He had found it very difficult to accept John's sexuality. Guess it went back to his upbringing, which has so much to answer for. It is so sad he had not allowed that love to flow to his sons in those formative years. Maybe it just needed time.

CHAPTER 27

Although our weekends—especially Saturdays with the boys' sporting activities—were busy, John was keen for us to have a beach house on the Sunshine Coast. Like me, he loved Alexandra Headland. He was excited for us to have our own place to escape to. He had been acquiring a lot of clients in Brisbane who had properties on the coast, and they were keen for him to manage them. He knew the boys would love it and we could all be together. He coasted the suggestion with the idea I might also get some rest time. I never found his devotion smothering; it was a great feeling to have someone care so much for you.

So, the hunt was on. John came up with three units, all dog friendly, with the help of a local agent, Judy, who he had come to know. One was a holiday unit belonging to a Melbourne family; the agent told us we could stay in it overnight and look at the other two the next day. The boys were excited and packed their bags straight away.

We all loved the unit immediately upon arrival. It has three bedrooms, an outside courtyard, and was close to the beach ... and wow, looking down the road we could see the surf. That's all we needed. The boys couldn't wait to get to the beach, so John told them to get ready and they would go down.

John looked at me with no smile. "Here are the weekend papers. Come sit outside, and I will get you a gin and tonic. Don't move. We'll get fish and chips tonight, old man." Then, I got the smile.

The boys all came back wet, sandy, and happy. I think the decision had been made. I queried with John whether we could afford it. He responded with a smile, "All sorted."

We settled in for the evening and the other inspections were cancelled. Judy told John, "Knew you would all love it."

After a month, it became our beach retreat and although it was fully furnished, we changed some things, installing bunks for the boys. They were delighted and soon sorted out a roster for the bunks. We had never, ever, heard our boys argue, however, they chided and teased each other all in good fun. The weekends at the coast were special, and I often joined the boys at the beach, as my man had several takeaway favourites. Our beach stays were resting time, and I was barred from the kitchen. Geez, how was I going to get to the fridge for my chocolates?

By now, there was a need to establish an office on the coast, and John asked me what I thought about appointing Todd as a manager. John had taken him under his wing, and he was going great guns. John could travel between the coast and the city when needed and stay at the unit if needed.

"Great idea, John, go for it."

He beamed.

Todd had broken up with Pat, who had decided he needed something younger. They had not lived together but had exchanged unit keys. We were told that Todd had turned up at Pat's earlier one day, because an open house had been cancelled at the last moment and found him in bed with a young guy. Pat roared at him, said he was spying on him, and told him to piss off. Todd threw the key at him, went home, called a locksmith, and turned up on our doorstep in a mess.

Todd was elated about the move; it would be a new start for him. He and John went up to the coast and, with the help of Judy, found a small shopfront with a one-bedroom flat upstairs. Todd was in heaven. They came back so excited with John showing me all the photos and asking what I thought.

"Looks great, but you can make the decision. It's your business."

"No, it's our business; we always make every decision together."

"It looks great. Go for it. Looks like the flat upstairs desperately needs a coat of paint though, and possibly new carpets."

"You and Todd sort that out, okay? You know that stuff."

Some days later, John wanted to take me and Todd back up to see the shopfront and then, if we all agreed, the contract would be signed.

We indulged in social chit chat on our way to the coast, when Todd told us a gay client had hit on him. He really liked him but thought accepting a date with him may be unethical during the negotiations. John indicated that once the transaction was completed, either settled or did not proceed, that opened a possibility to meet up.

Todd replied, "Thanks Johnno. I never thought that would happen when you are doing business."

"It has happened to me over the years, but I just ignore it."

"You've never mentioned that before, young man."

"No need to, just comments I ignored. If they got a bit persistent—which always irritated me—I just said, 'When the fridge at home is always full, who needs takeaway?'"

Silence.

John reassured me, "It was nothing, babe."

Laughing, I had to say, "Thought that was the best comment ever. You'll be taking over my job next."

"Never! I've read everything you have ever written; you are my teacher. Gonna pull over and kiss you."

"Keep your eyes on the road, young man, and keep driving."

"What's a fridge got to do with getting off?" came from Todd.

"Toddy, stick to takeaways!" John and I exchanged a wink.

So far in life, Todd had been unlucky in love. He always seemed to find the wrong guys. After Pat, he had a series of boyfriends, but they never lasted long, because Todd, like John, wanted the romance as well. I always told him it would happen. Heavens, I had waited fifty years!

Todd eventually took up with the property client after settlement. The relationship went well, but the fellow always came to him and seemed to be secretive about his life. He never invited Todd to his home. Todd asked, but Tim said he looked after his sister, who was divorced and had children. Todd accepted that, but one day, Tim left his phone at Todd's place, so Todd decided to drop it off at Tim's work. Tim was a builder.

Dropping off the phone, the lady at the desk said, "My husband loses his phone all the time. I wonder how he ever gets his work done. Thanks."

Humiliated, Todd walked out and texted Tim to call him.

After about two hours, Tim rang Todd, saying he and his wife had an open relationship. Tim just thought having a wife may put Todd off, and he still wanted Todd. He wanted to meet Todd to explain. They met. Tim said sex with Todd was great. "So please, let's keep going as we have. Let's explore more. I love you and want you so much. My wife means nothing to me, but you do."

Todd shook his head and said he had been told so many lies that he didn't trust him. Tim threw him a lascivious look. "I want you now." Tim lunged at him, ripping at his clothes as Todd fought back. Being strong, Todd took control.

Tim just glowered at him, and slapped his face with, "You were dull sex anyway, just a gay faggot slut." He turned and walked out, laughing.

Todd arrived on our doorstep, as he had before, a mess. Sometimes, you just keep on learning lessons.

But life often opens opportunities when you least expect it. Maybe there was someone waiting in the wings? Yup, wait for it ... Todd told us he had been invited to a school reunion but wasn't interested in going. It had not been a happy time for him, struggling as he grew up confused about his sexuality, but being such a good football player at school, he was spared many questions.

John and I urged Todd to go to the reunion, but he procrastinated. After that we did not hear any more about it.

About two weeks later, Todd rang me. "Hi Robbie, can you, Johnno, and the boys come for a barbie on Sunday?"

"Sure, that would be great. We will bring wine. Anything else?"

"No, just my favourite men."

I queried with John if he knew if anything was going on. Had Todd mentioned if he went to the reunion? John said he had forgotten about that, but Todd said nothing and was his usual happy self.

Sunday came, and we arrived at Todd's, to find a man there who we were introduced to as Adrian. He was short, lithe, wore glasses and was nervous. We settled down for a drink, and after the usual pleasantries, Todd suggested the boys might like a swim. There was a pool in his unit block, so the boys took off.

Todd and Adrian seemed a bit on edge, so I broke the ice. "Guys, are you okay? Are we making you nervous?"

"No," said Todd. "A lot has happened since the reunion, and I am so pleased you wanted me to go."

John couldn't wait. "What happened? Did you guys know each other at school?"

"No," replied Adrian, "we knew each other by sight and name, but that was all. Todd was ... I guess you would say ... I felt he was like my big brother at school, although he didn't know it." We both looked at them, confused.

"I'd better explain," Todd said. Looking at Adrian, "Okay?" Adrian nodded.

I may have been dreaming, but in my view, the eye contact said it all.

Todd told us school was not easy for him. He saw boys who did not meet the macho image—those who didn't play sports and the like—they enjoyed the arts and similar things, so they were scorned. One fellow he remembered was Adrian. All the blokes joked at his 'poofy' name, derided him because he was short, and looked like a nerd. Todd felt sorry for him and told the guys to lay off him.

Adrian jumped in. "You cannot believe how good it was to have someone stand up for me. No one else ever did, so I really liked Todd. However, in reality, I knew a macho footballer wouldn't look twice at me. Why would he?"

We asked Todd if he liked Adrian at school. He didn't think about it because he was so caught up in keeping his private thoughts and sexuality under the radar.

Todd told us Adrian had contacted him out of the blue and asked if he was going to the reunion, but replied he was not sure. Adrian told him he hoped so, as he always wanted to thank Todd for being there for him. School wasn't a happy place for him either, but Todd was good to him and helped him ease through the bad bits. Todd said he was taken aback by that revelation. This guy was thanking him. It was the first time that had ever happened.

Todd admitted with a blush that when they met at the reunion, it was as if he had seen Adrian for the first time. They just kept talking like old friends.

Adrian told us that he had seen Todd had come out, so hoped his wish would come true as he admired Todd so much. Todd blushed, took Adrian's hand, and told us it did that night, and they had spent two weeks really getting to know each other. Todd admitted no one had ever treated him the way Adrian did, except (looking at us) you two! Laughing, he claimed, "But you two are my sisters!"

Someone declared, "Bubbles!" as two noisy boys ran in, dripping wet.

Well, I must say we were happy. Adrian was a lovely man and wow, what a couple they made. I don't think we had ever seen Todd so relaxed; it was like he had grown up overnight. Adrian had harboured a love for Todd since he first saw him and had shown him such kindness. He secretly felt he had been under Todd's wing all that time at school, which was what kept him going.

We were so pleased to see our friend in love and happy. Sometimes, finding the right person just takes time.

CHAPTER 28

Routine domestic life carries on for everyone, and its very nature gave us the comfort and security we desired. Our family had settled into ours, with very few disruptions, and we enjoyed the contentment of it.

Friday night was always special for us; it was pizzas and a movie of the boys' choice. It wasn't always what we wanted to watch, but as they grew older, we hoped the boys' choices would improve. They did, however, like John, love James Bond, so every month or so, we were saved. The boys relished in the action, but their comments were priceless. What children observe! "Why does he like his drink shaken and not stirred?" asked Liem.

"Cause," claimed Huy, "he's not like Bo and Dad, who like bubbles just as it is." Peals of laughter from the boys. Just gotta love children.

Dare I say it ... well, we often watched my favourite, *Sleepless in Seattle*, after they went to bed. Admittedly, John never ever said he hated the movie, though I know he did. But he always indulged me. I don't know how many times we watched it before I told him, "No more! I know that you hate it."

"No," he told me. "Soppy as it seems, I just love watching *you* watch it. That's far better entertainment than the movie!"

So, I pushed the young man out of bed. Strong athletic footballers always recover.

One Friday night was more memorable than others. I heard John's car come in at a fast pace; the car door slammed. The door from garage to house slammed. The boys, who were doing homework, looked up when a very angry John walked in. "You okay, John?"

"No! Need a stiff drink!"

"Boys, Dad has had a stressful day. How about you finish your homework in your room, and I will call you when dinner's ready, okay?"

"Yes, Bo," they nodded at my suggestion.

"John, sit down, drink on the way."

I handed him a drink, and he gulped it down in one go. "Top up?"

"Yes, you have one too, double gin with tonic, and sit with me."

Sipping our drinks, I waited for him to talk.

"You know that fucking sleazebag cop, Pat? He called me today. 'Hi Johnno, how are things? I thought that it would be good for us to catch up,' he said."

John looked at me. "How he treated Toddy was bad, but I thought, okay, we can catch up. So, I said, 'Yeah, Robbie and I can catch up with you.'"

"Well, I thought it would be just us," he continued. "Thought you might like something younger. We could have a bit of fun, you know, be a change from an oldie. There's nothing like younger guys for a good time.'"

I raised my eyebrows but kept silent as John continued.

"Then he made a fucking gross comment. What an arsehole. Fuck Robbie! I cannot tell you I felt like shit by that comment. How could he think anyone, let alone him, would tempt me from you? I was so fucking angry, my hand clenched into a fist. I just shouted, 'Piss off!' and hung up. If he had been in the room, I would have decked him for starters."

Putting my arm around him, I murmured, "John, calm down. He was just being a sleaze. We know how he treated Todd. They just try it on. He seemed an okay guy when we first met him at the hospital. He is out of our lives now. Anyway, what did he say?"

"Nothing of consequence, just made me feel sick just listening to him."

"Go on, tell me, I'm grown up."

"No, I won't."

"John, remember no secrets."

"Okay, well, you asked for it. He said, 'Robbie always looked like he would be crap sex.'" John laughed. "Boy, did he get that wrong!" and gave me an intense hug.

"John, he's just the type to try it on with anyone; probably gets lucky every now and then. Forget it; it's more a reflection on him. Poor Todd, he really fell for him, and he was his first. That's always hard."

"I know a lot of couples have open relationships, and some of our friends do, but I never wanted that. I can't tell you how much I love being with you; it just keeps getting better."

"Everyone is different, and people make their own choices, but we found what we wanted, and we have grown together. There's no need to explain that to anyone. Come on, cheer up, you go and play some ball with the boys, while I get the pizzas ready."

"Love you. Remember, no anchovies on mine."

I chuckled to myself. I found, if you minced them up finely, no one ever knew.

Over the years, I had learnt how sensitive John was. He was tough on the field, but he was 'soft' in his heart. He was very hurt that someone would even think he would cheat on his partner. People think it's an oddity these days, but it's not. Out there in the real world, people still find deep love.

In many ways, John had a lot of his father in him, and a wonderful loyalty in his love for those he cared for. Tony, his father, was tough on his family and, although he struggled to understand John's sexuality, he was totally loyal to his family. Speaking to me at the party must have been the toughest thing Tony ever had to do. The way we are brought up can have a massive impact on our lives. It can define how we think.

John's older brother suffered, but Ginge broke out. He was lucky to have the strong support of his wife, and to his credit, he knew that.

CHAPTER 29

Away from work, our lives now revolved around the boys and their school activities. But life always has hiccups. John and I had learnt that the hard way and had managed to protect the boys as much as we could as they were growing up.

Meeting them after school was a ritual I enjoyed. Sometimes, this was with John, though on occasions we would allow them to walk home with their friends, thus giving them some feeling of independence.

Life can be bumpy, stormy, and even cyclonic when you least expect it. One particular day is etched in my memory. I noticed the boys came out of school and instead of lots of chatter with their usual greetings, they were much quieter. I ran with it. They took Toby's lead, and we walked. No chatter.

"Guys, you seem quiet today. Everything at school, okay?"

"Yes Bo," they chorused.

"Guys, I know you both so well, something is up. You know how we always talk about things, get things out in the open, so please let me in."

I watched them look at each other. They worked as a team.

"Bo, what's a 'poofta'?" asked Huy. I stopped and stared at him. He saw my face. "Did I say something I shouldn't Bo? Sorry."

"No Huy, you didn't, but why do you ask about that word? Come on tell me, what prompted this? We need to talk."

They looked at each other and then looked at me. Liem answered, "One of the boys at school said we had two dads. We told him yes. He asked why and we said our mum and dad were killed in a car accident and our dads were our family now. He said his dad said our dads were both pooftas and dirty men."

I am not often short of words, but I was stunned. Catching my breath, I replied, "Guys, we need to talk. That word is a 'derogatory' word, which means it is a disrespectful and nasty word to describe a man who likes men. People who don't understand the people they are talking about use it. Tonight, at home, we will talk this through with Dad, so you understand that this boy's dad is wrong. Sometimes, you can have two dads or even two mums if they love you. Dad and I love you both very much and Dad and I love each other. Come on guys," I announced with my throat tight. "Time for a cuddle, then home."

I think they gave me the most heart wrenching cuddle I had ever been given, with Toby leaping about to join in. As we walked on, I added, "Guys, do you want to talk any more about it now or did that help? We will talk about it with Dad tonight."

The twins laughed. "Bo, you always make us feel better." God, love my boys.

I knew we were in for a night that hopefully, we would help solve such issues for the boys in the future. I knew we would all learn from this.

John came home, and we had our evening drink together. The boys always finished their homework while we had 'our' time. It was a special time each day. I acquainted John with the afternoon's events. He looked grave. "How are they?"

"Good. I think I defused it for now, but we need to jointly talk to them so they always feel that when any issues arise, not just of this sort, they can open up to us."

"It sounds as if you have laid a good foundation for us, my go-to man. Always there for us, beautiful husband. Glad no one ever hears us talking. 'What soppy romantics those guys are,' they'd say."

That smile.

"How should we handle it, Robbie? This is all new to me. Shall we wing it? That has served us well for all these years."

The boys came to get their non-alcoholic drinks and joined us. John asked the boys what they had learnt at school that day. They responded, as always, with school chatter, and I watched the three of them nattering together. I never get tired of it.

"Guys," said John, "Bo told me what happened today at school, so I want the four of us to open it up, discuss it, then bury it. Okay?"

"But Dad," said Liem, "we talked with Bo, and it's all sorted."

"Yes," confirmed Huy. "All sorted."

John looked at me, and then at them. "Guys, we want to make sure there is nothing lingering in your minds about it. It was a nasty word to describe us, but in using that word, I think it says more about their dad than it says about us."

They told us it didn't matter.

"Bo told us a funny thing that people say, 'Sticks and stones may break my bones, but words can never hurt me.' He told us that if someone calls you something nasty, it cannot hurt you."

"He was right. As you get older, you will both find that happens to everyone and you just ignore it."

"We do," replied Huy. "A few weeks ago, someone said we were just 'chinks', but we both laughed at them, and said, 'Yes'. We've been called that many times before, and we have a song and dance we perform for them."

They stood up and danced as they sang, "We're just a couple of funky chinky boys, funky chinky boys, funky chinky boys."

They rocked with laughter. John and I were astounded. How resilient are children?

Leading up to when the boys turned fourteen, John had chats with them about issues they would come up against in life. The sex education and drug issues were dealt with at their school, as well in programs developed by the school. Nevertheless, we encouraged the boys to expand on what they had learnt and ask us anything that they still didn't understand. They were open about all they had learnt, and they seemed to have no issues that confused them.

In such a digital age, so much is out there. But we kept up our talks with them after each of their school sessions; we wanted them to know we were there for them to discuss anything at all, no matter what.

CHAPTER 30

Meanwhile, John's real estate business grew; he had a natural talent for it. Even his father, Tony, was full of praise for him, which made John so happy. John had always sought approval from his dad, and our glitch—well, a big glitch—was now behind us and their relationship was so strong.

John was very pleased with how Todd had developed as an agent. He, like John, was so personable that he grew a large client base. Both had been well respected in their football years, which put them in high standing.

My days were kept busy and not often interrupted until the boys came home each day. One day, however, just another, ignites in my mind. The boys were about fifteen when a call from the school principal alarmed me. She said Huy had collapsed, and the ambulance had been called. She asked if I could collect Liem and go to the hospital at Smithfield Street.

I shuddered. *Oh, that hospital.*

I told her I was on my way. Driving to the school, I rang John and told him what I knew and said I would meet him at the hospital. As I pulled up, I saw the principal walk out with Liem, who was crying, "Huy's sick." The principal expressed concern and indicated she was not sure what had happened.

Liem jumped in and we sped to the hospital. I quizzed Liem, and he burst into tears, saying, "Those dope guys made him take a pill."

I went into a cold sweat, my hands on the wheel dripped water; I felt I was choking.

"Bo, are you okay?"

Composing myself quickly, I nodded, "Yes Liem, I'm just worried about Huy. I'm sure he will be okay."

On reaching the hospital, John rushed to us, hugging us both with, "Oh God, this hospital."

John said the doctor would be with us soon.

"Liem, can you tell us what happened so it will help the doctors treat Huy?"

He looked at us both. "Will we be in trouble, Dad?"

"Telling us helps Huy. Helping people doesn't get you in to trouble, okay?"

Liem looked at us both and nodded. "Well, the dope guys ..."

"Hang on, Liem. Who are the dope guys?"

"We all call them that cause they always make trouble, Bo. They're always trying to get us to buy pills from them."

"What sort of pills?" asked John.

"They say they make you feel happy, but we keep refusing. They called us fags, sons of pooftas, no- good for anything, just sissies who cannot take a man's pill.

"Huy got jack of them and took three, I think, but he put them in his pocket and walked off. I followed, but they were yelling and screaming at him. So Huy screamed back, "I'm a man!" Then he swallowed one.

"Huy yelled out, 'I don't feel anything; they're fake pills! About twenty minutes later, he passed out."

John jumped up, "Stay here."

Ten minutes later, he came back. He said he had told the doctor what had happened, and that they had found two pills in Huy's pocket. The hospital promptly sent the pills for analysis. The doctor said Liem's input was a great help and John hugged him for a job done well.

John looked at me with a frown face saying the school had rung the police.

"Robbie, I just hope that scumbag has retired."

As we turned, we saw Detective Sergeant Patrick O'Reilly come out of the lift. A saying I love about 'gin joints', floated through my mind.

"It'll be alright, John," I stated, as I stroked his back.

O'Reilly walked over to us. "Hi guys, small world."

John glared at him. "Liem and I are going to get Robbie a coffee." Taking Liem's hand, they marched past him.

'Our' policeman fixated on me. "Johnno's just the same, pity."

I decided to stay silent. He then moved on to see, I presume, the doctor.

What happened all those years ago at Smithfield Road Hospital flashed through my mind, giving me a feeling that chilled my spine.

My boys came back with my coffee, which gave me some strength. We decided not to alert the family at that stage. We had enough to deal with. Huy needed to recover, and we needed to keep an eye on Liem.

John looked drawn, so I told him he needed a laugh. I told him what flashed through my mind when I saw O'Reilly. I got a small smile, but it was a weak one.

The doctor came over with O'Reilly hovering at a distance. The doctor said he had told O'Reilly he always talks to the family in private and waited until the police officer moved away.

The doctor looked at Liem and said gratefully, "You did some great detective work there, young man. It was very helpful. We will make your brother well again." Liem beamed.

The doctor revealed that as only one tablet was taken, it was a bonus. The results showed a mixture of drugs—none of which were harmful—but when combined, they could produce various reactions. Fainting was one, so if the patient had any heart issues, the outcome could be serious.

"I am sure your boys have learnt a valuable lesson. If the police want to talk to you, then get your lawyer. One of my older and very valued nurses remembers you both from years ago and explained what you had to deal with. She said she was sure seeing the same policeman again would bring back painful memories." *Are you kidding?!*

Sitting there with Liem, John and I were drained. The concern for our son was paramount, but the hospital brought back the past. We had moved on with our family and our sons, but the past always lingered in the background. Things dim, but never disappear. Everyone lives with that. The doctor advised us to go home; he felt Huy would be able to be discharged in the morning.

It was a quiet drive home and the next morning, an early call from the doctor saw us on the way to pick up Huy. He certainly looked much better, hugging us as we went to the car. Huy was full of remorse, but John and I explained to him it was an experience to be learnt. "Put it behind you and move on."

The boys did not go to school that day and we decided that we needed another pizza night. That always put my boys on a high. Time to move on, yet again.

CHAPTER 31

It never rains, but it pours ...

A few weeks later, John's phone rang one evening. We saw him listen, his face grave with, "Very sad, we will be in touch."

Shaking his head, he sat down, took our hands saying, "Sadly, Ong Noi has passed away peacefully this afternoon."

As the news sunk in, tears began to roll down the boys' cheeks. They hugged us and sobbed. Words don't help at these times but holding them tightly gave them comfort. It was the last link with the past for them, bringing back the loss of their parents so many years ago.

It was a quiet occasion at the funeral home. It was just us, the boys, and Clare. We chattered about the good times with him, encouraged the boys to talk about the times with their parents and Ong Noi. We never wanted to take them away from their family. We wanted to help them keep their memories till that curtain closed.

The boys wanted to mix his ashes with those of their parents, which Ong Noi had kept. They would take them to scatter in the hills in the north of Vietnam, where they all came from.

Clare joined us for lunch at our favourite Vietnamese restaurant, which was a fitting send off for a cherished man. Later at home, the boys were quiet, and we let them have their space. A very strong link from the past had evaporated.

John and I settled on the sofa, a platter of cheese and a drink in our hands, with only candles burning around the room. We had heard the boys earlier in the pool, then saw them sitting and chatting away; they needed their alone time as did we. As dusk arrived, they came inside and curled up with us on the sofa. They just wanted to be with us in silence.

CHAPTER 32

The years kept slipping by, with lots of cherished memories created along the way.

The boys finished school and were now adults. It was time to decide a future. The boys were so close; they talked with each other always, and we were all so bonded. We helped them to decide what they would like to do in the future.

Huy decided he wanted to be a doctor and Liem liked the idea of a nurse being at the grassroots level of health. They expanded on this with us and said, "You have always encouraged us to work together and you, as our dads, have set us that example. We love you both and will prove it to you."

We approved of them in taking these paths, so their chosen careers awaited them. John and I were so proud of them. We had sons who were career driven, and to be honest, we loved them. What dads wouldn't be?

One night over drinks, they told us that they hoped we would understand; they both had a dream to go back to Vietnam and work in a hospital in the remote area where their parents were born and raised. We were overwhelmed by their sensitive, caring nature.

John saw the tears in my eyes and taking my hand he mumbled, "Guys, Bo and I support you in everything you do. We think that is a wonderful dream and know you can pull it off. It's a wonderful venture that you want to achieve in

Vietnam. Always our boys, but now you are men going out in the world. Wow, we will drive you crazy with our visits."

We all laughed as we sipped our drinks, and John popped another cork. *Geez, more bubbles!*

From then on, the house was always busy. Both boys would bring home friends from university for study and parties. We wanted the boys to do this and got to meet their friends so they could party in a safe environment. The boys' friends were all like them, students who wanted to achieve, and they all admired the boys for their dream of Vietnam.

We also received feedback that they thought we were the coolest dads and, of course, the footy fans all bragged to their dads about meeting John. There were quite a few autographed photos given out, but no autographed novels. *Geez, them's the breaks!*

Both had girlfriends and, like all young ones, these came and went. After a while, Huy seemed to be steady with a lovely girl called Lauren. We came to know her and even had her parents over for drinks, a barbie, and the like. They seemed comfortable with us, but we noticed we never got invited to their place. Well, Huy seemed happy, so we let that one drift.

We did notice though Liem had a new one each time and John thought he was the randy twin. I wondered as I watched him with each new girlfriend. Saying nothing, I allowed John to enjoy his thoughts.

One day, Liem was home before Huy and joined me in the kitchen as I prepared dinner. He seemed to want to linger, and I guessed he had something on his mind. He fiddled around, made a cuppa, then suddenly said to me, "Bo, can I ask a strange question?"

"Sure, fire away."

"Well, I wondered, well thought, like, if you met someone, and um sorta like them, but think you like being with them, is that like in love or just friends? I guess what I'm asking is ... what if it's not a girl, but maybe a boy?"

I thought this was a moment to draw breath and draw on all my resources. "You mean like Dad and I?"

"Yes, how do people know if they like someone of the same sex? I mean, I am just curious to know, you know. I like girls. How did you know you liked Dad; you know ... I mean loved him?" Liem blushed.

"I think we told you we first met at Jimmy's birthday party, and I didn't know he was a famous footballer, but he thought that was funny. I didn't think much about him, but he wanted to go and have coffee with me, which I thought was odd. I was curious as to why he kept wishing to talk to me, so I agreed. Straight away, he opened his heart up to me."

"Did you fall in love with him then, over coffee?"

"Heavens, no. We had some misunderstandings in our communications, but despite this, we kept seeing each other and he made it clear he liked me, but more than just a friend.

"I was concerned about our age difference, but he said that was no issue for him. I guess I enjoyed being with him, then missed him when he was not around. We gradually grew close together. The first time he put his arms around me, I felt warm and happy. It seemed just right. I found when I looked into his eyes, we seemed to look inside each other. Does that make sense?"

"Yes, I think I understand, but won't ask about the physical bits," Liem laughed.

"That's okay. Your dad and I have always had a loving physical relationship and I have to admit, it never dulls."

"Oh no, Bo, way too much information!"

"Maybe talk to Dad too," I suggested.

"Okay. Just curious. I have a girlfriend," he added.

I smiled inwardly.

Later, John came up behind me in a very chirpy mood and put his arms around me.

"Liem asked me, 'How do you know if you really liked someone, maybe loved them?' I told him about us, how meeting you changed my life. I knew you were special and from day one, I wanted to be with you, although I had to work on you!"

"What, young man?"

"Only kidding. I did have to do some groundwork, but knew it was worth it. Told him it was so hard to explain, but when you know, you know. So, do you think he has someone in mind? He hasn't brought a girlfriend around for a while, so he must be keeping her hidden away."

I am running out of inner smiles.

CHAPTER 33

I was working on the last of a series of short stories for a book that I had been asked to contribute to. The phone interrupted my thoughts, and I saw it was my nephew, Jimmy.

"What's up Jimmy?"

I heard him sobbing on the phone.

"Jimmy what? Tell me. Jimmy, please."

"It's Mum; she's gone. Massive heart attack."

I could not comprehend what he was saying. "Jimmy ... what?"

"She's gone, I can't talk," and the phone went dead.

Still not wanting to believe what I had heard, it cannot be true. I slumped over my desk and broke down, sobbing.

I was so distraught; it didn't register that John should have been at work when he rushed in and wrapped me in his arms. He grabbed the phone, and finding it dead, dialled.

"Jimmy, I'm home. We'll come over and see you and your dad as soon as the boys get home. But right now, I need to comfort my man."

He looked at me explaining, "Jimmy rang me and asked me to come home because he didn't want you alone when he told you."

I couldn't stop sobbing. Ruth and I were so close, it was as if my guts had been wrenched out. I felt desperately alone, shaking as John and I clung tightly together.

"Robbie, we are always here for each other. Come on, let's lie on the bed, and talk when you feel you can."

I don't know how long we lay there; memories of Ruth flooded my thoughts. Suddenly I thought ... no more Ruth calls! I laughed, then cried.

"Robbie?"

"Just memories flashing through my mind, John. All those calls from Ruth—especially in our early day—and I always thought, *Oh no, not another one!* Now there will be no more. At the time, I didn't think that one day I would miss them." I sobbed as my man hugged me.

We heard the boys come in and John dashed out to them. I heard them talking before they all slowly came in. The boys were crying as they climbed on the bed and threw their arms around me. Auntie Ruth was special to them and was always there for them. We just all held each other, not saying a word. John sat on the bed, stroking my leg. His touch was warm and comforting. How such a simple touch can bring so much solace. After a while, the silence was broken by Liem. "We loved Auntie Ruth so much."

"Yes," agreed Huy. "She cared for us."

Then silence again.

Sometime later, John suggested showers, then we would go over to see Barry and Jimmy.

❍

Jimmy hugged us as we arrived, and Barry came straight to me and hugged me. I was nonplussed; never in all the time I knew him did I ever receive more than a handshake. Ruth had always said to me no one ever saw the real side of Barry. She was always so happy with him ... I finally guessed why.

We went inside, engaging in small talk. John said if everyone agreed, he would order pizza and we could just sit around and chat, then drink a toast to our Ruth. I called out, "No anchovies, John."

"Yes, Robbie makes the best pizzas with no anchovies."

I could almost hear a chuckle from Ruth in the silence.

The doorbell broke the subdued mood, and Jimmy ushered in John's dad, Tony, with a bunch of flowers. He walked straight up to me and handed them to me with, "She was a tough one, but always on your side."

Turning, his fist tapped John's shoulders, "If this one ever treats you bad, come to me."

With that, he turned and left. There was a hush and then, when John started sneezing heavily, I handed the flowers to Huy, who hurriedly took them away. I had learnt very early in our relationship that the pollen in flowers had this effect on John, so his flowers of choice for me were always a 'bouquet of chocolates'. I often chided him that he must want to fatten me up, and he replied that he would always keep me well and truly exercised. *Blush.*

That night, when we crawled into bed, John wrapped his arms around me with the go to sleep message of, "If you need to talk during the night, we can."

Sleep came slowly, but the heavy breathing of my man holding me tightly eventually brought it on.

Like everyone, I felt I was in a wasteland until the funeral was over.

CHAPTER 34

The boys kept me busy over the next few weeks and said they would be at home Saturday night for a family barbie. Like all young people, they were normally always out and about. Huy said he was bringing a new friend, Lisa, home to meet us. We asked what happened to Lauren. He explained she wanted a future husband to be in Australia, not Vietnam. She had no interest in the boys' dream, so with a look of sadness, Huy said he had to accept he could not be happy if he couldn't achieve his and Liem's ambition. We understood.

He said he and Lisa had gone out a few times. She was two years below him in medical school and she had revealed to him that she thought his aspiration was fantastic. He said they really got on well, and he realised he had more in common with Lisa than Lauren. But it was early days in their relationship.

Saturday afternoon came, and the barbie was all ready to go. John and I were sipping our drinks as Huy arrived with Lisa, together with Cadeo, a Vietnamese medical student. We knew Cadeo well, as he was one of Huy's best friends.

Huy introduced us to Lisa. She was short, curvy, and had a smile that came sort of close to my man's, though it certainly was not as spectacular. I had to say that didn't I?! As a bonus, she had a bubbly personality.

As we laughed and chatted, we both observed Huy's attachment to her. He was smitten; he was so at ease with her, which we had not noticed in him with Lauren. It would go well.

I asked Huy where Liem was. Laughing, Huy replied, "On his way."

John and I exchanged glances. *Did he have a surprise for us?*

Shortly after, Liem called out, "Hi everyone," and walked in alone, sitting himself beside Cadeo. They grinned at each other before Liem laughed, and taking Cadeo's hand, stated, "Bo, Dad, meet my boyfriend."

John and I were gobsmacked. It was not often we were both lost for words. We never saw it coming, although I suspected there was something in the wind, but never Cadeo.

"Liem, thank God, I can relax now," shouted out Huy and we all laughed.

John and I got up and hugged the boys. We had always liked Cadeo. He was a quiet, studious young man—the glasses helped—with a soft nature like Liem. *Wow!* John put his arm around me saying, "Congratulations guys, Robbie and I are so happy for you both. Wow, what a surprise." I winked at Liem.

Before he could continue, and in unison, Huy and Liem shouted, "Bubbles!" as the four of them fell about laughing.

We asked them how it came to this. Liem deferred to Cadeo, who spoke. He said he had known for some time he was gay and when he met Huy in first year, he introduced him to his brother, Liem, one night at the pub. Cadeo liked Liem and knew he wanted to get to know him, but didn't know if he was gay. He felt uncomfortable asking Huy if his brother was gay. He watched Liem going out with girls, so he thought all was lost. But then, he noticed that there was always a different girl, so he stayed friendly when they met up.

Liem interrupted. "I was getting the feeling that I wasn't attracted to girls but liked looking at guys. I wondered why every time I saw Cadeo, he was smiling at me, making me feel comfortable. I enjoyed his company, though I couldn't explain it to myself. When I saw him, I got excited in a way I am a bit embarrassed to say."

"Horny Liem! Just horny!" shouted Huy.

We all laughed, and John answered with, "Liem, that is only natural when you are really attracted to someone. I won't tell you the effect Bo had on me!"

The room was full of "Oh my God, too much information!"

"Time to top up the drinks to cool everyone down," I announced.

Huy laughed out loud.

John and I felt truly blessed. Sitting there drinking altogether, we watched the bond so visible between the boys and their chosen friends (it was a bit too early to call them partners). I looked at my man, we clinked glasses and John whispered to me, "We did well," with that smile.

Nevertheless, we could see Liem and Cadeo were a little on edge. I guess the coming out announcement was a big thing for them, so we wanted to make them feel as comfortable as possible. I patted John's knee, and he came to the rescue with, "Cadeo, relax, have another drink and stay the night. No driving for you. We don't have many beds, so you will have to bunk down with Liem, okay?"

Huy laughed heartily, "Really Dad, always too much information. Really!"

John blushed. Still that sensitive man. Cadeo smiled a thank you. Our family was growing.

Liem still looked nervous. Finally, he came out with, "We want to talk to you both about Cadeo's parents."

In all earnestness, Cadeo took a hold of Liem's hand, "My parents do not know I am gay and are very traditional Vietnamese people. I don't think they will react very well. From comments they make, I know marriage to a girl is what is expected, and nothing else. But I cannot do that. Now, with Liem, I know he is who I want to be with. We have been seeing each other for a while but wanted to be sure before we told you both.

"Huy and Lisa caught us out together a few times, so they guessed what was happening."

Huy interjected. "I told them to get on with it and tell you, I couldn't be happier for them, but his parents will be an issue."

I asked Cadeo if he had brothers and sisters and he said a brother and sister, both a bit older and married, so the pressure was on.

"Cadeo," I said, "do you have a good relationship with your brother and sister? Can you talk to them?"

"Yes, Mr Burke but—"

"Drop the Mr Burke Cadeo, call me Robbie. We are family here."

"Well, that's settled, and I am Johnno. Only Robbie gets away with calling me John. That's the way it's always been, and always will be."

"Cadeo," I said, "we got off track, sorry, but we solved something important."

Cadeo continued. "Robbie, Johnno ... my brother and sister are always urging me to go out with the girls that they line up for me. They tell me it's my duty to marry. My brother even said to me, one day, that I wouldn't want people to think I was a dirty queer."

He looked as if he would burst into tears.

John said, "Cadeo, I know this is an odd, perhaps inappropriate question, but do you think your family would be more comfortable with the fact your partner is of the same ethnic background?"

"Dad!" exploded Huy.

"Sorry, just starting the conversation."

"Thanks," said Cadeo. "I know you mean that with good intentions, but Liem would need a sex change for them to accept him. I will just have to deal with it."

John reached out and put his hand on Cadeo's shoulder, "Cadeo, we are all here for you both. You are not alone. I think we have another journey ahead of us. Robbie and I already know the highway."

CHAPTER 35

The boys' study came to an end, and they settled into their relationships while John and I watched on with great comfort. It had been an amazing journey for us, and it was far from over.

Liem had graduated and was working as a registered nurse. Cadeo continued to study to become a doctor, though he was still struggling with how to deal with his family. We, together with Liem, told him not to admit to them he was gay until he was strong enough to deal with the family reaction. We could see the grief it was causing him, so we rallied around Liem while he cared for Cadeo. We made sure we supported our boy and his partner.

They announced one Friday they were going away for a weekend. We told them the unit at Alexandra Headland was there if they wanted it, but they said no, they were going to Byron Bay. John and I exchanged glances, fondly remembering our sojourns there. Later, I expressed concern to John and hoped all was okay. John laughed and made a comment they were young. It would be a romantic getaway.

That weekend was a quiet one for us; Liem and Cadeo were away, and Huy and Lisa were at her parents' for a family dinner. John prepared a barbie, and we sat on the veranda with some drinks, reminiscing, but always the Cadeo issue came into our discussions.

Late on Sunday, I was in the garden while John was working on real estate projects when Liem and Cadeo arrived. I knew at once something was wrong. They both looked wretched and Cadeo had been crying. They came up to me and my arms circled them both as they sobbed.

"Come on and sit down and tell us what's going on." I called out to John to join us. As we sat down, John came in and, from his expression, I could see his concern.

"Are you boys, okay? Not an accident? Please, tell us."

Liem hugged Cadeo. "No accident, I will explain." He looked terrible.

"Take your time, boys."

Slowly, Liem told us that they had decided to go away somewhere they had never been to and discuss how to deal with Cadeo's parents. Cadeo told Liem he wanted to marry him and spend their lives together. If it meant being ostracised by his parents, he would have to accept that. He could see no life ahead without Liem.

Cadeo's parents were still giving him some financial support, and he knew that would end immediately. They both had part-time jobs and because Liem had now graduated, he had a good paying job.

Cadeo interrupted with, "I told Liem I would not have him support me."

Liem chimed in: "I gave him an ultimatum. If he wants me to stick around and marry him, I am the breadwinner until he graduates."

Cadeo cried.

Reaching out, Liem took Cadeo's hand. "Cadeo, I love you and want to be with you forever, so please just accept this and the day you graduate, you can buy me the wedding ring."

We all dissolved. Another 'not a dry eye in the house' event.

While they had been in Byron Bay, Cadeo had phoned his parents, telling them and his siblings he had something he wanted to discuss. He and Liem then drove from Bryon to his parent's house.

Upon arrival, Cadeo's family was all there. Cadeo introduced Liem and said he was the brother of a friend from university. He told everyone he knew his news would be hard for them to accept, but he wanted to be honest with his family and tell them he was gay. Also, he wanted Liem to be his partner.

They all remained silent, looking at the thunderous face of the father.

The father stood up, pointed to the door and said, "Go, I will have no son I acknowledge like that. Leave!"

Cadeo looked pleadingly at his mother while his brother and sister turned their faces away from him.

Sadly, he took Liem's hand and walked out. With a heavy heart, he realised he was leaving a lifetime of family memories behind.

Outside on the footpath, Cadeo took Liem's hands and hugged him, reassuring him: "It's just us now."

John and I wiped our eyes like a couple of sentimental oldies. It was so emotional watching our son become a man, supporting the one he loved. We knew good things had rubbed off. We insisted they stay with us to save money; we could turn a couple of rooms downstairs into a studio for them, which would give them privacy. They responded gratefully, with heartfelt hugs.

At that moment, Huy and Lisa walked in, bottle of bubbles in hand. "Why the sad faces? Someone cark it?" Talk about a night.

We shared Cadeo and Liem's news to bring Huy and Lisa up to date and to make sure we all were on the same page. After that, Huy reassured the couple: "We are family, Cadeo and Liem. Together we will move forward, all united."

CHAPTER 36

After Huy and Cadeo had both graduated, the boys announced they wanted a low-key double wedding in our garden. It would just be the four of them with us and Lisa's mum, Shirley, as the bridal party, family members, a few of their friends, and of course, Clare, who had always kept in touch with us all. Sadly, Lisa's dad, Roger, had died recently.

We sat down with the four of them and Shirley to plan. We decided on a simple wedding with Vietnamese finger food. I was outnumbered in that they all wanted it catered. They all agreed I had to relax and enjoy the day.

I announced there was a special Vietnamese dish often served with families gathered for *Tet*—the Vietnamese New Year celebration. "I would like to see that served as a celebration," I declared.

"Tell us about the dish, Robbie."

"Well, it is Thit Kho, a braised pork dish with eggs. Small portions could be served at the beginning with a fork. Easy to make beforehand and keep hot. It is a special treat to start the wedding breakfast and a very traditional meal."

Liem piped up. "How about we let you guys decide on that one, okay?"

They all agreed, then left for Shirley's for a night.

That night in bed, we negotiated. John was great at tactical manoeuvres, but I had a few tricks up my sleeve. So, the negotiations commenced. I must confess we enjoyed it more than we should have and eventually John capitulated, far too early, I thought.

Sometime later, we both fell into a deep sleep. The next morning, as I awoke, he turned to me. "Do you want to negotiate who gets the morning cuppa?

Sternly, I looked at him." No negotiations, young man; you!"

"Spoilsport." He smiled and walked out. Tea was served accompanied by a chocolate. I think he is here to stay.

The boys arrived for breakfast unannounced. "Hi guys, what's up?" asked John.

Huy smiled. "We wondered how the negotiations went."

"Well," said John, "Bo kept me up all night negotiating."

"Oh, no!" exclaimed Huy. "Too much information, guys. I bet Bo won. You can't say no to him, Dad."

"Well, Bo and I agreed we would cook it together and the other food would be catered. It's our way of very much being part of the wedding, and I love that."

The wedding day came, and our friend Trish arrived to officiate. Shirley, John, and I, greeted all the guests as they arrived together with Lisa, Huy, Liem, and Cadeo. In keeping it simple, and with a nod to tradition, Lisa wore a red three-quarter length silk dress with gold embroidered collar. The boys wore long-sleeved, white embroidered shirts with black silk pants.

Overcome with emotion, John welled up and squeezed my hand. Wow, did they all look a knockout! It was certainly different from Spiderman and Wonder Woman!

John could not contain himself with his mum, dad, and family—and for the first time at a family event—his brother, Tony Junior, arriving for the wedding. It all takes time. They all walked in, hugging us all.

Sadly though, Cadeo's family would not come, even though invited.

The wedding proceeded, followed by both couples kissing to rousing cheers and applause. Lisa spoke about her mum and late dad while jokingly, Huy then thanked Shirley for entrusting Lisa to him. Cadeo thanked John and me for the warm welcome we gave him from the start, expressly appreciating the support from us both during the difficult times with his family. In Liem, he knew he had found his soul mate.

Then there was silence as Liem and Huy stepped forward to us and took our hands. Solemnly, they spoke.

Huy: "From the day we came into your lives, you took care of us."

Liem: "You both embraced us as your family."

Huy: "That never wavered."

Liem: "We remember that first night, we never felt lonely again."

Huy and Liem: "We wanted to give you something to mark this day, but no object could express our true feelings for you both."

Huy: "We rang Clare to ask her to the wedding and told her our dilemma."

Liem: "She told us she had the perfect gift and told us what it was."

Liem and Huy: "We are going to ask Clare to give it to you."

John and I were totally bewildered.

Clare stepped forward and faced us:

"I congratulate the boys and their partners. I had the pleasure of introducing the boys to you both and I knew a strong family would grow out of it and it has. It was a pleasure to be with you all and watch how you grew together. Although I'm retired, I never wanted to lose touch with your family.

"I now have a confession. Although I needed to meet up with you on a regular basis as part of my job, I always made excuses to catch up more often. When Huy and Liem mentioned they wanted something special, I had the perfect answer. I had a story to tell Johnno and Robbie. However, it was a story that was classified in departmental records. My old boss was still working, so after a lot of negotiations, I was given permission to tell this story, on this very special occasion.

"Johnno and Robbie, you remember going to meet the boys' grandfather, Ong Noi, that first time?" She looked at us and we both nodded. I expect we were both wondering what was coming.

"You spent time with him and that was the first stage. After some hiccups and discussions with him, I went to see him for his answer. He told me, 'Yes.' I asked him if there was anything that sealed it for him. He smiled at me and said, 'Yes, there was.' He told me his daughter- and son-in-law—the boy's parents—were a devoted couple and he loved watching them together. When they looked at each other, they always smiled, but more importantly, their eyes lit up. He said he saw that in the two of you, so he knew."

I slumped into John's arms, overwhelmed to have received that blessing from Ong Noi, even now, so many years later. His arms tightened around me, and I knew he felt the same.

CHAPTER 37

After the wedding, the boys and their partners put in place their move to Vietnam for work. They wanted to settle in the northern area where their parents came from. After some research, they found no small clinics in that area, so the idea of a small country hospital did not eventuate. Instead, they settled on the large hospital in the province of Bac Kan. It was a large hospital, servicing remote areas nearby.

They obtained the appropriate visas and secured the job positions. Eventually, the day came to take them to the airport. In some ways, their departure was sad, but assurances we must visit often comforted us. Their absence would just make our home so silent.

Fortunately, John's business was still growing, and he was kept busy, as was Todd and their colleagues. I was fortunate that work rolled in at a good pace, so we were both kept busy.

We had an online Zoom meeting once they had settled into Bac Kan. It was great to hear all about the hospital and the accommodation they had. Each had a small unit in the same building. It was within walking distance of the hospital, but they told us they were looking at getting a second-hand car for trips on their days off. They would also use it for sightseeing with us when we visited.

About a month later, they invited us to come up when we could. As this was in November, they suggested Christmas so we could all be together.

John exclaimed, "On to it guys; gotta book tickets." He promptly left the Zoom meeting and off he went.

I raised a smile to the four of them and they laughed. "Gotta love our dad. Bo, tell Dad we will arrange a hotel."

I said my goodbyes and joined John, who was in a 'sea' of flights. I placed our diary in front of him.

Next stop ... Bac Kan.

❍

Arriving after the flight and a crowded bus trip north, we were greeted by the four of them with lots of hugs and kisses. We piled into their car and drove to the hotel. Huy laughed and said, "It's called the 'Green Hotel', nothing environmental about it, just painted green. Our flats are too small, and we know you like your space."

John and I did not exchange glances.

We quickly checked in and were whisked off to Huy and Lisa's flat for afternoon tea. We saw Liem and Cadeo's flat first, before sitting down to the delicious treats Lisa had prepared. Yes, the flats were small, but the two couples were happy in their own first homes.

Excited chatter followed when Lisa suddenly announced, "Robbie, Johnno, you are going to be grandpas."

We looked at them, stunned, unable to cry, then we burst. The place was in an uproar. Someone said, "I guess it's bubbles time!" Did we laugh! The baby was due about May. John had the iPad out.

"John put it away. Don't book the flight yet." No smile.

Lisa explained they would keep us posted but wanted us to visit again before May, and she wanted us to bring her mum, Shirley, up. We didn't hesitate, immediately nodding our 'yes'. They told us they wanted us there for the birth. John's smile had not been lost.

We took them out to dinner that night to celebrate, even though we were tired. I had suggested to John that we have an overnight stay in Hanoi to draw breath, but he wouldn't hear of it. "Robbie, I can't wait for us all to be together again." I wondered if he had plans for an office up there.

We had a wonderful week with them, and Christmas Day was planned around their hospital shifts. We only had an hour when all four of them could be with us. We had arranged for the hotel dining room to do local food and drinks for us, at that time, which would be our Christmas dinner together.

I loved it. I announced I was writing a travel article to show that Christmas was about being with loved ones wherever you are and sharing the local food. We know the boys greatly appreciated this rather than turkey or pork. (Although beforehand, I quietly told John dinner was his choice, the first night home.)

John and I had never exchanged expensive Christmas presents. Approaching our first Christmas together, he told me he wanted to surprise me, but didn't know what to get me. I think we both knew that our strong relationship was our gift, so I told him to surprise me ... but nothing under ten thousand dollars!

He was unsure, then seeing the glint in my eye, he beamed. I received a pair of gold y-front jocks filled with my favourite chocolates. He was determined to fatten me up!

He cracked up at the t-shirt I gave him. It said: I CAN'T LIVE WITHOUT MY ANCHOVIES.

After that, we had the best Christmas presents ever. I must confess our boys thought we were weird, but hey, let's just say it again: we're hopeless romantics.

❍

We managed to squeeze in one more visit to them in Bac Kan with Shirley before the actual birth.

John and I were counting the days leading up to the birth of our first grandchild. Todd told me everyone in their office, as well as their clients, knew it was close and were happy for us. People just loved Johnno.

When we had an anticipated date, John booked the flights. I was happy that we had a date; it calmed him down. If we had to wait up there, so be it.

So, our departure came, we flew out, and arrived in Hanoi to a text: 'It's a boy! Sorry guys, Roger couldn't wait. He arrived early. Roger wants to meet Grandpa and Bo-pa.'

We hugged each other with sheer excitement. The staff in the immigration department seemed confused about two Aussie men completing formalities and continually wiping our eyes. With that behind us, John flagged a taxi, negotiated a price and we were off to Bac Kan; no way was he going to suffer a long bus ride to meet Roger.

We arrived at the hospital, bags and all, to meet the boys. We went straight up to Lisa and Roger. John wasn't going to be held back. Talk about a little prince. As John held Roger, we thought he would never give him up.

Over the years, I have seen so many of John's emotions, but this was extraordinary. John wept as he cuddled him. I didn't think I would get a look in, but when I did, John hugged me so tight, so he was close to Roger.

We spent the whole afternoon with Roger and Lisa; the boys had their rosters.

Lisa said she and Huy had agreed he would be named after her late father. Shirley would be so pleased. When the nurse came in and said it was Roger's rest time, we continued to chatter away while keeping our eyes fixed on our grandson. No need to say again, but he really was a beautiful boy and, like John, Huy was the proudest dad.

It took the nurse some effort to prise us away, but we knew both mother and son needed their rest. Tomorrow was around the corner.

We had dinner with Liem and Cadeo; Huy was on a shift and any spare time he had was spent with Lisa and Roger. The boys updated us on life there: working in the hospital; bike rides in the area; and visits to family in Pac Ngoi.

Cadeo told us he randomly sent emails and texts back to his brother and sister, telling them about his life in Vietnam. Sadly, he had had no response, so far. He looked at us sadly. "One day, maybe. I just hope it's not too late."

Liem comforted him, adding, "The other thing is, we are finding adoption up here harder than we thought, but we are persevering."

John and I glanced at each other. We both knew Roger's arrival had brought all this to the fore.

It was a wonderful week with them all and especially having time with our grandson. John insisted before we visited that he oversaw presents for the baby. We (unknown to Huy and Lisa) came up with some that were for a girl and some for a boy—to cover the odds. So, Grandpa and Bo-pa left him with a football and, of course: a koala, several t-shirts, a mini-aussie felt hat, and baby nylon swimmers, seen on every Aussie beach, which made Huy convulse: "That's my dad!"

John had taken, I don't know how many photos—of guess who—to show back home as well as those he had shared on WhatsApp. Maureen texted us: 'The headlines back here are—*Johnno Willadoro a Grandad.*' And I thought our interest was fading.

Flying home, we clinked glasses filled with guess what?! John smiled at me and with a sigh stated, "I know it was hard for us in the early days, but I always knew we would have a wonderful life together. And it just got even better. Wonder if the next one will be a boy or girl?"

"Give them a breather!"

CHAPTER 38

Despite the newest addition to the family, life after Ruth left an empty hole in our lives. I had John, the boys had their partners, and Barry and Jimmy spent more time with us—which we enjoyed. I did wonder about Jimmy, though. He didn't appear to have any steady companion. Both he and Barry seemed lost without Ruth, with Jimmy providing a constant shoulder for Barry.

Barry had always seemed so distant, but I now saw Ruth had been his rock, and was possibly Jimmy's as well. They both adored her, becoming almost inseparable since her death.

We included them in much of our activities. John was amazing in embracing my family. Curiously, his family also seemed even closer to us after Ruth passed. I have her to thank for that. Maybe she laid out the path. She was so grounded in family, and in reflection, I understood what she had hoped to achieve for us all. A united family was her dream.

I had loved Ruth so much. She was tough, yet so loving. After Ruth died and the twins were living in Vietnam, John and I suggested a joint family visit. It would include Tony, Merryl, Ginge, Maureen, Barry, and Jimmy. Surprisingly, everyone jumped at the idea. I said to John, "OMG, what a tour that will be!"

He laughed and agreed. "You will be in your element."

"Big hug needed, young man."

So, our two families flew out to visit the boys in Vietnam. The boys were amazed when we told them, but embraced the idea. We all landed in Hanoi for an overnighter before getting ready for the trip to the north. I must confess that on arriving in Hanoi, I had never seen my family and John's family so excited. Barry and Tony chattered away like old friends, laughing and joking together. *Ruth, did you engineer this?* She would have loved it. Watching them all so happy on arrival made her absence so obvious.

I had explained to them the accommodation would be basic, but that didn't seem to bother anyone. We had arranged rooms at the Green Hotel, where we had always stayed on our visits. They all lapped up this new experience. I said to John, "It's like a group of scouts at camp!"

Laughing, he exclaimed, "Pulled it off again, my man; hope we have to share a single bed!"

"Watch it. You could end up sleeping on the floor!" He smirked.

The week went well. Everyone enjoyed catching up and Roger was one spoilt boy. How many koalas does a boy need?! Roger had arrived early, a boy on a mission, and has never stopped moving.

Jimmy, Tony, Barry, and John played ball with the young patients in the hospital. I had never seen them so happy, and Tony even said to me, "When are we coming back?" Wow! How times change!

Even John's mum, Merryl, who was always so quiet, except with a bubbles in hand, was into the crafts with the young girls, together with Ginge's wife. Heavens, we may be moving here!

The only sad note was Tony Junior, John's older brother, who did not come. He said it was not for him. None of us really understood him.

I was concerned about the food. I thought John's Italian family background may have been an issue for his family, but they embraced the Asian food.

After telling me, "I'd done well for his son," John's dad, Tony, was finally warming to me. I knew he loved John very much and was proud of him. Through subtle comments he made to me since that chat, I realised he had come to understand his son. He watched him create a family, and like Tony, family was so important.

Tony and I had a great unspoken working relationship, for which I was grateful, especially for John's sake. A close, loving family was what John lived for and what we both wanted.

We decided to do some sightseeing during our visit, so the boys had arranged a local tour guide and minibus. Every second day was a tour.

One trip was to the Ba Be National Park, about seventy kilometres from Bac Kan, so I knew it would be a full day. We were told it centred around Ba Bể Lake, which means "Three Lakes" in the local Tay language. It is a very large natural freshwater lake, stretching about eight kilometres in the north-south direction.

On arrival there, we stopped at a small food stall for tea and coffee before some exploring. It was lovely to be out in the open and enjoy the rolling hills. The limestone cliffs were amazing, and we saw different vegetation than we were used to.

About noon, our guide led us to Nhà Hàng Phúc Khánh, a little eatery overlooking the lake. Our guide had told us to make sure we enjoyed such local specialties as Ba Be grilled fish; roasted suckling pig; chicken; five-colour, sticky rice; steamed bamboo shoots with meat; and sour shrimp sauce. He mentioned the corn wine, a typical drink of Bac Kan province. It is fragrant, gentle, sweet and reputedly, if you are drunk, it does not bring on fatigue and headaches like other alcoholic drinks. We all decided on a local beer instead.

After lunch, we had a boat cruise on Ba Be Lake and up the Nang River to the Puong Cave, which is noted for being the home of ten thousand bats. I opted to stay on the boat in the cabin with the door locked! I must confess, bat caves do nothing for me, but the troops enjoyed it. After a long bus ride home, we all crashed into bed. Even John was snoring before I could say goodnight. Is that a first?

On our last day, we rested up for the journey home. Lisa took Meryl, Maureen, and I shopping in the town, including the massive Vincom Plaza. I just carried the shopping bags.

It was always sad to say goodbye to the family there, but we knew our visits would continue.

CHAPTER 39

Several months after the trip, John's dad died suddenly. John was devastated. They had a rocky road during his formative years, and it hit rock bottom when he met me. However, over the years as our family grew, Tony mellowed and not only embraced John, but me and the boys as well. The boys loved him and loved all his visits when they played together. I once told John that Tony should move in. But I got a look that screamed, "No!"

The boys flew in for the funeral; they were deeply upset. They said they had a few days to spend with us, so I suggested that after the funeral, the four of us go up to the Bunya Mountains, north-west of Brisbane. John loved having the boys around and it would be a serene place to relax. So, we set off. Arriving at the cottage we rented, John and the boys stoked the fire while I prepared dinner. We sat around the fire reminiscing until sleep came.

Next morning, we set off for one of the walks with backpacks full of goodies. Walking along in silence, John took turns with an arm around each one of us, wanting the warmth of his loved ones with him. We stopped, every now and then, for snacks or when the boys spotted various birds. That, of course, was camera time. They soon had John involved. I could see his mood lighten and a sense of relaxation cloaked the four of us.

Back in the cottage around the fire, we all tried to identify the bird photos against the bird book in the cottage. Amidst the disagreements, the result was a lot of laughter.

That night in bed, John's cuddles became tighter. I knew how much he needed me.

Older family members slowly faded out of our lives as we and the boys grew older, so our family grew smaller. It was a part of life we all had to deal with. But through the boys, our family grew.

CHAPTER 40

Over the next few years, John and I visited the boys regularly. Huy and Lisa gave us two grandchildren, adding a daughter, Linh, arriving a few years after Roger. John and I revelled in being granddads.

On what was to be our last visit to Vietnam while Liem and Cadeo were there, Liem and Cadeo told us they had decided to move back home. They were finding it too difficult for two men to adopt children in Vietnam. Huy and Lisa were saddened by this, but they understood; Liem and Cadeo were entitled to have a family.

Cadeo and Liem told us they were working on a date to move back and had investigated a place to move to, but wanted to make sure it was all in place before they told us.

We were ecstatic to have them back closer to us.

They told us they had been in touch with a doctor who ran a small clinic in the town of Millurat, in Southeast Queensland, about three hundred and fifty kilometres from Brisbane. Excitedly, they told us we could visit every weekend if we liked.

Cheerfully we responded: "Relax, we will give you some space." John added, "You need space to start a family."

"Dad really; geez!" declared Huy.

An older doctor and local nurse ran the small clinic. He was struggling with the workload and wanted someone to take over so he could ease back. The boys, being a doctor and nurse, were perfect, plus they liked the idea of working in a small town.

Also, they pointed out it was great from an economic point of view. The government offered good incentives to medical practitioners who were prepared to relocate to small, regional towns.

Liem and Cadeo had Zoom meetings with the doctor and the nurse, revealing at the first meeting they were a married same-sex couple, which prompted a reply, "Country people are very accepting."

Cadeo said in subsequent Zoom meetings, the doctor had told them that patients were being advised of the proposed staff changes, and the town was planning a big welcome party.

We could see the boys were excited but knew Huy and Lisa would miss them. Huy and Liem were always a team.

CHAPTER 41

Finally, the day arrived when Cadeo and Liem flew in, and we met them at the airport. We brought them home for the night with the expectation they would drive to Millurat, the next day. We wanted to drive out and help them settle in, but they insisted, "No." They wanted time to settle in; then we could visit.

We understood; we were just excited to have them back.

Next day they left, and later we received a call saying they had arrived, and the welcome reception had overwhelmed them. They told us there was a one-bedroom flat at the back of the clinic that the doctor and his late wife had used when they first set up. They had later built a house.

The flat had not been used for a long time, so tradies and locals had all pitched in to freshen it up. Cadeo and Liem arrived to, what they felt, was a palace. Have to love country folk.

We were so pleased but itching to go out and visit. I have more patience than my man who loves to get on with it. I opted to give him a non-anchovy pizza on a non-Friday night. He was distracted, but only for a short time.

His patience only lasted a week! I told Cadeo and Liem if they could cope; I needed to bring John up for a visit as he was driving me crazy with his longing to visit them. I asked if there was a local hotel to book us in. They laughed and told me to bring him up. Getting off the phone, I called out to John, "Start packing. We're off to Millurat, first thing in the morning."

He rushed in, holding a suitcase. "Packing for both of us, you get dinner."

Needless to say, as we climbed into bed, he was sound asleep in seconds. I prepared myself for his fidgeting to wake me about 4.00 am.

I managed to drag out the departure to 5.30 am under the proviso that we had a breakfast stop on the way. No smile. So, at about 5.30 am-ish, with John waiting in the car, motor running, we left. I did get my breakfast stop briefly, though I had to tell him not to gulp down his food.

We arrived at about 10.00 am following another forced coffee stop where again, I didn't receive a smile. But upon our arrival, Liem and Cadeo's welcoming smiles greeted us, much to our delight.

The boys introduced us to the doctor and his assistants at the clinic. We found they were a united group. We headed off to the hotel to check in and meet our host, Bob, the publican. Over the next few years, we would come to know Bob well. John was in seventh heaven.

We spent time exploring the township of Millurat and the surrounding areas, spending our evenings with the boys. They loved what they were doing and had so much to share with us. John and I were so happy to see them settled, happy, and loving their work. We were contented to leave and were told in no uncertain terms they wanted more visits any time. John remained happy.

Over a couple of years, our visits to Millurat continued while our Zoom meetings with Huy, Lisa, and the children kept us up to date with their family, though we still visited them. Our family meant so much to us.

CHAPTER 42

It was a lazy Sunday afternoon in Brisbane; John had a big launch of a unit project in Brisbane, the night before, and insisted that I go.

The developer, for whom he did a lot of work, and his wife, always wanted me to attend their functions. Maybe we were still that famous same-sex couple or that they just loved having us both there; it seems the people who came to these launches enjoyed our company. So, the next day, we relaxed. John was working in the garden and had developed a passion for orchids; I was working on my latest novel.

About mid-afternoon, I felt a pair of arms engulf me and a whisper in my ear, "Let's have an early sundown drink. It's been a big week."

We poured our drinks and moved into the garden. John always turned his mobile sound off at these times. He said it was our time. If the screen lit up, he could choose whether to take it or not. We sat enjoying being together and chatting now and then. We enjoyed just being together.

When the phone lit up, showing Liem's face, he picked it up.

"Hi Liem, how's things?" He listened, his face grave. "What? Tell me ... I'm putting you on speaker ... Liem, I can hardly understand you. What's happening, son?"

Liem was weeping and got out in a garbled voice that Cadeo had collapsed. He was on oxygen, unresponsive, and shortly the emergency helicopter would be on the way to take him to Prince Charles Hospital in Brisbane.

John told Liem we would meet him there. "But what has happened, Liem?"

"We don't know. I'll meet you both at the hospital."

John and I rushed inside, changed, and John called a taxi. We did not need a breathalyser on the way. Arriving at the hospital, we waited for the helicopter to arrive. As parents, they were still our boys. We waited.

After about twenty minutes, we saw a team of doctors, nurses and Liem with the trolley being wheeled into a room. One of them spoke to Liem. He nodded and rushed over to us, hugging us. In between sobs, he told us they were starting extensive tests, so we needed to wait. We sat back down and Liem looked at us straight in the eye and gulped, "I didn't like what I saw." The despair that was written on his face was heartbreaking.

We reassured him, and he slowly settled.

Liem told us he had sent a text to Cadeo's bother, Nguyen, to tell him what had happened. We looked at him with uncertainty, wondering what had transpired. He explained after they arrived back in Australia, Cadeo had sent a text to his brother asking how they all were and giving news of their return to Queensland. Cadeo received what he felt was a warm response. Nguyen added he and his sister, Mia, hoped they were both well and enjoying their new life back in Millurat. The texts continued on a semi-regular basis so they hoped sometime, in the future, when they were in Brisbane, a reunion with them might be possible.

While we were chatting, we saw a couple walk in and presumed it was Cadeo's siblings. Liem immediately stood up and went over to them. We had never met them, but Liem had, on that one occasion. Liem brought them over and introduced us as his dads—Johnno and Robbie. We all politely shook hands while Liem explained what was happening.

Nguyen and Mia were visibly upset. Nguyen said to Liem, "My sister and I have been discussing a reunion with you both lately. We very much regret not defying our father's wishes. We are greatly distressed that it has taken this to bring us to this point. We hope we get to reunite with Cadeo, as well as yourself. If not, and we hope it is not the case, we will carry that for the rest of our lives."

Just then, the doctor appeared and came over to Liem. "Tests are progressing, but we suspect that he has suffered an aneurism. It is in the part of the brain that makes it all a bit tricky. I don't want to be the bearer of bad news, but it is serious, and we are pulling out all the stops. He has the best team working on him, and he is young and healthy, so we can expect a positive result."

John put his arms around Liem as he started to sink to the floor. We all sat down in silence as the doctor walked away. I could tell everyone was numb, like me.

Small talk doesn't work at times like this; it always seems innocuous, as if just skirting the real issues.

John suggested, "Maybe a coffee for everyone?"

We gave him our orders, and my arm around Liem replaced John's. It took me back to the days when the boys were young, and they needed a cuddle. Liem seemed just like that little boy in my arms, seeking a dad's comfort. They never really grow up.

Coffee came and for a while it broke the ice. Nguyen asked Liem if he enjoyed living in a small country town. Liem opened up, eager to take his mind off what was engulfing him. We all joined in and, for a while, we escaped the darkness surrounding us.

A beep on Liem's phone brought a sigh of relief. 'Huy and family have landed in Sydney. They will be here in about three hours.' I thought, *Liem will survive*.

We saw the doctor walking towards us, and we all knew it was bad news without him speaking. His face said it all. He looked at Liem, "I'm sorry Liem, it's over. We did everything possible, and my team are devastated."

Liem spoke quickly. "Can I spend time with him?"

"Yes, come with me."

John called, "Liem."

"No Dad, I want to be alone with him."

We sadly watched him walk away as John circled me with his arms and we sank to the seats. Taking a deep breath, Nguyen looked at us. "We will sit together for a quiet moment outside his room so we can say goodbye after Liem comes out."

Feeling overwrought, I sought guidance from the expression in John's eyes.

"No Robbie, we will remember him as he was. You don't need it. My memories will be as with yours." Always united, so many hurdles, however, so many trophies.

When Liem finally emerged from the room, he looked a shadow of himself, totally wrecked by what had transpired.

Looking at each other, the three of us felt adrift with nowhere to go, swimming again in that wasteland.

John, always to the fore, always a leader, suggested we all go home and spend time together. We asked Nguyen and Mia to join us. To our surprise, they accepted.

However, a distraught Liem looked at us. "If we leave here now, that brings it all to an end."

What can one say at a time like that? All words are empty.

John put his arm around Liem. "He will always be in our hearts, Liem," as we slowly walked out, leaving a life behind, memories just all boxed up.

CHAPTER 43

As we sat around, bereft of our usual cheerful banter, we heard car doors and two noisy children. Liem walked out as Roger and Linh ran in, calling out, "Grandpa. Bo-pa."

We jumped up to hug them, only to all end up on the floor as Huy, Lisa, and Liem walked in. Liem introduced them to Nguyen and Mia. Huy shook their hands in a formal manner as did Lisa. The twins had both displayed soft natures, but Huy was black and white in his approach to evaluating others. He was very angry in the way Cadeo's family treated their son, his good friend, and his brother, Liem. This relationship would need some work.

As we shared our deep sorrow with Huy and Lisa, Nguyen and Mia excused themselves, saying it was time for us all to be together. That certainly took some heat out of the room.

After Nguyen and Mia left, we all sat down with a drink while the children happily rediscovered the toys that we always had in boxes for them. Despite the reminiscences abounded with emotion and laughter, Liem told us how numb he felt. He was unable to take in what had happened in the last forty-eight hours. Although we were all close, John and I knew having Huy there was the comfort he needed. John ordered in takeaway, always mindful of support for me. Liem told us he would sleep on the day-bed on the veranda. He didn't want to sleep in his old room because it held too many memories.

Sinking into bed with John, both of us were tearful as his arms comforted me. It was a fitful night of lost sleep, his snoring actually serving as a reminder that my man was close beside me.

We arose early and saw the boys deep in conversation outside, so we left them.

Meanwhile, we made tea and poured juices for our little ones who ran out for morning hugs. Lisa wandered into the kitchen, insisting on making breakfast, so we had playtime with our grandchildren. We mucked about, cheerfully ignoring the spilt tea and forcing out the awful memory of the last few days.

When Lisa called the boys in, we all sat down to platters of fruit, eggs, bacon, and toast. Lisa made more tea and coffee. As we grazed with our tea and coffee, Huy said he and Liem had something to tell us. We looked at them expectantly, with Huy confirming, "All good."

Huy revealed that he and Lisa had been discussing for some time about moving back. He smiled as he saw the pleasure in our faces. They felt that schooling would be far better here, and they admitted they missed us, Liem, and Cadeo, very much. They had planned to talk to Liem and Cadeo about working out west, preferably close to them.

The events of the last twenty-four hours had accelerated the planned discussion, so this morning, Huy had run the idea past Liem. Liem beamed. After Huy told him of the proposal, Liem realised it was perfect; his clinic would now need another doctor. What a possibility.

Lisa chimed in, "We do miss you all very much, especially Robbie's pizzas ... without anchovies, of course. That nailed the idea!"

We all laughed, and Lisa winked at me. I like that girl.

Liem had been in touch with the clinic the whole time all of this was happening, and a locum doctor had been flown in to cover. Liem had also been in contact with the hospital board to organise a replacement for Cadeo, recommending Huy. Lisa's skills as a doctor would add an extra incentive. After discussions by Zoom, the Board said they would come back to them as soon as they could.

Leaving the boys to oversee the arrangements for the funeral and staffing of the clinic, we offered to take the little ones to the park. We took off, picking up coffees and juices. Our park was yet again a haven. John and Roger tossed and kicked a ball around while I helped Linh with her colouring-in book. We stopped for our drinks, then went back to kicking a ball and a colouring book—a princess in a fairy-tale castle. *Pity life isn't always a fairy-tale.*

Next day was the burial. Liem wanted a simple funeral and a brief service at the graveside. As we walked to the open grave, we saw Nguyen and Mia standing there. Huy left us to go over to them and speak. He shook their hands, hugging them both before leading them over to us. John and I looked at Liem in surprise.

"I said nothing. My brother always works in his own time."

John squeezed my hand.

After the burial, which was also attended by friends of Cadeo and Liem, everyone returned to our place. Lisa had arranged for some food from our local Vietnamese bakery. Lisa, John, and I kept busy serving drinks and food, leaving Huy, Liem, and their friends to catch up. We were pleased to hear some laughter as they remembered the good times.

Later, while Lisa and I were having a drink, she told John and me of their plans to move back. Being brought up in the city, she was excited to be moving to a small community and being involved in it. Her idea of a small country school for the children was a bonus; that would be good for them.

The next day, Liem and Huy were a bit slow. They had talked long into the night after everyone left. By now, they had set the wheels in motion for Huy to take up the doctor's position at the Millurat clinic.

Back at the hospital in Bac Kan, the manager and staff were disappointed to be losing Huy, but they understood. Cadeo had been held in high esteem, so much so, they planted a Tamarind tree on the grounds in his honour.

Later in the day, while we were enjoying some drinks, Huy's laptop lit up. Grabbing it, he and Liem rushed into the study, leaving us anxious to know the outcome of the job application.

After ten minutes, they came out grinning. Huy yelled out, "We're off to Millurat!"

Explosions of joy even though Huy told us he would be on a three-month probation period; but that was an expected formality. In unison, we all raised a toast to all being together again.

Huy and Lisa wondered if the children could stay with us while they went back to Vietnam to pack up. Huy would have a busy time handing over patients, and Lisa would have a hectic time finishing up her tasks.

After all this time, we were old hands at handling little ones. "Of course we will."

"Dad, Bo, you are always there for us. Lisa and I are so excited about the move."

"I have an idea. Why don't Robbie and I drive Liem back to Millurat, stay a few days at the hotel, as we do, and take the children? Huy and Lisa, are you happy with that?"

"Love it, John."

"We love it too," chorused Huy and Lisa.

Four questioning faces then turned to Liem for his response. "I would love that. Having all four of you with me ... it will make it easier to face those memories of that day we left. I'm not sure how I will go being in the flat back there by myself."

John came to the rescue. "We'll throw in some blow-up mattresses and all five of us can camp in the flat. The kids will think it's fun."

"Gotta love you Dad." Needless to say, the night ended on a high as much as it could.

Next day, John and Liem took Huy and Lisa to the airport while I entertained Roger with my football skills, much to his amusement. I gave Linh a camera to capture it all. Despite all the merriment, I certainly felt my age.

On their return from the airport, we started to pack all the things we needed for the trip. Liem wanted to go the next day; he felt he needed to get that first day back behind him.

Next morning, we loaded the car. I borrowed some old car seats from friends whose children had grown up. I packed the large esky with frozen meals I always had ready. Millurat had a small well-stocked supermarket; we would not starve.

So, we set off for Millurat, with Liem in the back seat entertaining the children. After a few breaks, we arrived about lunchtime at the clinic. The nurse and the older doctor rushed out to hug Liem and greet us. We were old friends after all our visits out there, and of course, Roger and Linh were the centre of attention. Roger did not object.

After leaving us to settle in, we unloaded everything, and Liem asked if we would mind if he went into the clinic to see patients.

"Of course. When you are finished, drinks and dinner will be ready."

That evening was quiet. Being in the flat forced us all to face those memories, but Roger and Linh kept the mood happy. Liem insisted we have the double bed in the bedroom; he would bunk down with the children. They thought that was wonderful. We guessed the bedroom held so many memories. It was going to be a tough road ahead for our son.

CHAPTER 44

Over the following twelve months, we had many visits to Millurat, always enjoying time with the family. Each time, we saw Liem become more contented; having Huy and family around was the best tonic. He was a doting uncle, which gave Huy and Lisa some time together. Life in Bac Kan had been hectic, and with two children around, they welcomed the change.

John and I noticed that not only was Liem happy and contented, but something else (which neither of us could put a finger on) was giving him that extra spark. We wondered if he might have someone new in his life.

We raised it with Huy and Lisa, who found it amusing. "You two are just hopeless romantics."

We left it at that, but we still held that thought. Time would tell.

When Liem and Cadeo got together, we were the last to know because he wanted to make sure. Whatever was happening, we were pleased for him. It took us back to our early days; however, our passion for each other still enveloped us, even if it was now a little less gymnastic.

Christmas was coming up, and I always made a big thing of it. With children about, that was special. We always liked to spend it together if we could, so after a regular Zoom call with Huy, it was decided.

Huy, Lisa, and Liem wanted us to go out to them for Christmas. They wanted to spoil us for once. We jumped at the idea. Lisa said she could never do roast pork and crackling like me, so it would be a leg of lamb. We didn't care! It was agreed we would arrive on Christmas Eve and stay until after New Year. We always stayed at the pub, which was a short walk to them. That made it easier for them and gave us some space. As much as we loved having children about, John and I did relish our 'alone' time together.

We arrived at the pub to be greeted by Bob the publican, who by now was a friend. "Welcome gentlemen, merry Christmas! It's an exciting one for you this year, enjoy. The key's in the door as usual."

After he disappeared, we trudged upstairs. "What do you think he meant by that, Robbie?"

"No idea, maybe because it's our first Christmas here, or he knows something we don't. You know small towns."

"Hey, maybe Lisa's pregnant."

"Doubt it, she always said two was enough and Roger's a handful. But I guess accidents do happen. Both boys are randy like their dad." Got a big smile, a big hug, and was thrown back onto the bed. Sometime later, we unpacked.

We took four cases out of the car and made our way to Huy's, just down the road. The front door swung open, and Roger and Linh flew out with squeals and hugs. Roger was right onto it.

"What's in the bags?"

"Just goodies for Christmas," replied John.

"No presents, Grandpa?"

"No, Santa brings those."

"Grandpa, get real. You need to Google that."

I wondered if there was any mystery left in the world.

Lisa and Huy came out with hugs and kisses. "Thought you would be here long before this," remarked Huy.

We both coloured.

He then joked at our embarrassment. "Too much information!"

We settled in for a drink after managing to hide the cases while John distracted 'Detective' Roger. While we chattered, Huy told us Liem was finishing off with some patients at the clinic and would be here soon.

Roger piped up, "We love Uncle Liem; he's the best."

I jumped to my feet, shouting, "He is the best," and striking a pose. There was laughter as Roger and Linh jumped and joined me in the pose. Over a few years, I had taught them a routine.

John put his hands over his face, "Oh no, Robbie".

But Huy hit the Spotify and out blasted, *The Best*. We were halfway through singing and miming when Liem appeared, followed by an older man. He was large-framed, well and truly a country man, holding his Akubra.

We froze. Liem introduced us: "Athol, meet Bo—one of my dads—and this is Johnno, my other dad."

We shook hands with Athol.

"Liem said what wonderful guys you both were, but I didn't realise you were so talented," said Athol amiably.

John joked, "I let him loose now and then."

Roger piped up, "Athol, do you realise you interrupted our song? I could have you arrested for that."

Playing along with the game, Athol pleaded, "I hope I won't go to prison!"

"Well," said Roger, "I'll put a good word in for you."

Laughter and someone announced, "We need drinks!"

It transpired that Athol was a friend of Liem's who lived on a property out of town. Athol accepted a beer; we suspected he was not a bubbles man. Athol told us he had looked forward to meeting us as he had heard so much about us.

John exclaimed, "Oh no!" but Athol remained friendly. "They're all good stories."

John and I exchanged a glance. We knew there was a story here.

Apparently, after Liem had returned to Millurat, and before Huy and family arrived, he often went to the pub each evening for meals. One night he walked in and Athol, who he had met a few times at the clinic, was there having a meal.

Following Cadeo's untimely death, everyone in town was being supportive of Liem, as both had been well regarded in the town.

Athol invited Liem to join him, which he did. In conversation, Athol asked him if he played snooker, which he didn't, so Athol offered to teach him. They played once or twice a week, with Liem taking to the game. Athol interrupted Liem.

"He was bloody better than me in a short time."

Exchanging a grin, Liem continued that Athol had asked him if he had ever ridden a horse. He hadn't, so Athol extended an invitation to his property one weekend, so Liem learnt to ride. That evolved into riding weekends. They both obviously enjoyed each other's company—from the constant eye contact—and John and I had a warm feeling. Athol was lonely on his property, and he enjoyed Liem's companionship.

Athol had been divorced for some years, and his wife and two children had moved to Brisbane. At that point, he seemed reluctant to continue.

Liem took his hand. "Tell them Athol; of all people, my dads will understand."

Athol scanned our eager faces. "Well, growing up out here can be tough if you don't fit the mould. In my teens, I felt uncomfortable around girls. I was an only child, so my parents wanted an heir. Sounds old-fashioned, but it's still out there. I remember reading an older book, *Maurice*, and found myself excited about the descriptions of Maurice and Alec getting together. I read those parts repeatedly, amazed by the feelings that it caused within me. I guess I found it exciting that books could describe such feelings between two men. I began to wonder, maybe I wasn't alone.

"But the pressure from my parents became so great, I couldn't see any escape, so marriage and children followed. I accepted my lot. My wife was a kind, caring girl and I guess it was lucky for me she wasn't overly interested in intimacy. When it was time for the children to go to secondary school in Brisbane, my wife suggested she move to Brisbane. She told me she thought I would be better on my own and we could both start new lives.

"We had really come to the point of just existing together. I wondered if she had guessed, however, she never said anything. We had never fought or argued, and in many ways in reflection, we were two companions sharing a house who just happened to have children.

"After the divorce, and as the kids got older, I told my son and daughter about myself, but they just commented it was my life. Cards, texts, calls have never been answered."

He looked expectantly at us and Liem. "I never went out seeking a male. I thought, *Who'd be interested in an oldie like me?*"

Clasping their hands tightly, Liem and Athol exchanged reassuring smiles.

"Liem and Cadeo had always been so friendly to me so, when I saw Liem come into the hotel for a meal, I didn't want him to eat alone. I just looked at it as a simple, friendly gesture. I thought the snooker might help him.

"I went home that night feeling happy, elated, but didn't know why. I thought he was just being friendly, but that was okay. I was happy to have him as a friend. As our dinners, snooker, and horse riding continued, I really enjoyed his company. I knew he was still grieving, so I did not want to jeopardise our friendship.

"However, I did feel there was a warmth growing between the two of us. I wondered about how I could give him a sign that I really liked him. I thought, *What could I do to make sure if he didn't want to go further, it wouldn't destroy our friendship?*"

"I had always been an avid reader from schooldays, so I remembered a passage from a favourite novel. I mulled over it and decided. After dinner and snooker one night, as we left the pub, I turned to him and said, "By the way, Barkis is willin'. I then walked to my ute and drove off."

I exploded with laughter. "That is classic, Athol, I love it!"

John stared at me blankly until I explained about *David Copperfield*. John turned to Athol. "You old romantic; a man after my own heart."

Liem had remained dumfounded outside the pub as Athol drove off. The words, *Barkis is willin'*, kept running through his head as he walked home. What was that all about? So, he went to his computer and Googled. What a discovery, uncovering the secret code. He felt a deep warmth. Not only was Athol a lovely man, but he was also offering an open door; no pressure on Liem.

He had become fond of Athol and very much enjoyed his company. He knew Athol genuinely cared about his feelings, and now he was reaching out to him, but at his pace. Liem had a sleepless night.

Next morning, he rang Athol. It warranted more than a text and all he asked was if they were they still on for horse riding and dinner the following weekend. Athol said yes, and Liem told him he would bring dinner.

"Liem, we're cliff hanging here. Spit it out," John groaned.

"Dad, be patient. Next weekend, we went riding and, after riding all afternoon, we freshened up and settled down for a drink. I told Athol I would get the drinks and came back with champers, flutes, and a bottle of Moet.

"Athol looked at me, unsure about what was going on. He's a beer man, as you know, but a gentleman, and watched as I popped the cork and poured two glasses. As we clinked, I said to him, 'Liem is willin'.'"

Sheepishly, Liem continued, "We didn't have dinner until the next day."

Athol welled up as we both hugged them.

Huy and Lisa, no doubt listening at the door, burst onto the veranda with Huy exploding, "Geez Liem, you dragged that out. Dad and Bo became eligible for the pension waiting!"

Amid laughter and hugs, John and I told them how happy we were for them.

They told us they wouldn't marry but had made commitments to each other.

"Johnno and Robbie, I cannot tell you how happy Liem makes me. I never dreamt he would want to be with an old bloke like me. I will always look after him."

Liem hugged him. John and I were so pleased to see our son so happy again. Huy rounded it off with, "Well, he's obviously got Dad's genes!"

There were howls of laughter from everyone except Roger who announced: "But Athol always wears his own jeans."

"Bo," continued Liem, "I always remember that time I asked you about relationships and how would you know if it was right. You said to me, 'You will know,' and I did."

I nodded tearfully.

"As I said, his Barkis comment let me know the door was open if I wanted to come in. It was a genuine proposal. Life has been good ever since."

Athol grinned but then said sadly, "We have not let this be overshadowed by my son and daughter not responding to my email telling them about Liem and myself. We accept that and have our future ahead of us. I know Liem and Cadeo wanted children, but Liem has told me that's in the past. Besides, Detective Inspector Constable Roger and Linh keep us busy."

That Christmas together was a wonderful, joyous occasion. Bob, the publican's forecast, was correct. Roger and Linh enjoyed all their presents, although Roger kept cross-examining Grandpa whether he had done the 'Google thing' that he was told to do. Grandpa—being a champion footballer—out-manoeuvred Roger, who eventually gave up his cross-examinations. Linh was much easier to deal with. *Just hope her brother doesn't take to training her. Somehow, I think Roger takes after his dad.*

CHAPTER 45

Days drifted into weeks; weeks drifted into years.

Life always brought up challenges, and I had noticed some changes in John's behaviour. They were just little things—an irritation at small things, asking me something, then again later, and sometimes looking at me with a vague look in his eyes. We were now in our fifties and seventies.

Out of the blue one day, he told me he felt it was time to retire. He had told Todd he was considering transferring the business to him, but until then, John would ease up his workload and work part-time.

"Robbie, we have enough to live on. We have good property assets."

I was stunned. It was the first time in all those years he had done something without discussing it with me first. I knew now, those behaviour changes were real.

"I did tell you I was considering this, didn't I?"

Ignoring that, I nodded. "I think it is a great move. We will have much more time together. Love it, young man." As I kissed him, my heart ached, for I knew now what lay ahead.

After that, we established a new routine of spending more time up the coast, visits out west, and at other times he pottered about in his garden with his orchids. His care for me never waned. But those odd behaviours kept getting in the way. Previously, if I had suggested Todd and Adrian were coming over, he would be excited. But lately he just replied, "Only us, please."

Conversely, Todd often asked us over, but John would say we were busy. I tried not to worry because it didn't seem to worry him until one day, when we were having our evening drink, he came out with it. "Robbie, I'm sure it's nothing to worry about, but I don't seem to feel the same. Little things irritate me for no reason, and I know I ask you things, several times. Worst of all, I get these periods of feeling incredibly tired; I don't want to catch up with people. Have you noticed?"

I needed to speak carefully. "Yes, I have noticed some little things like that. Maybe we need a holiday. That would allow you to slow down at work. We don't need the money and you own the business, so Todd and the other guys can step up, okay?"

"That's always a solution, but maybe I should see our doctor, just to make sure."

"I will make an appointment for us both to have a check-up. We are both getting older."

The following week, we saw Warren, our doctor, and outlined John's concerns. He questioned John about all his episodes and asked me for some honest observations. He said he would run some tests on both of us. That included an ECG to check our hearts. That would allow him to see if any more tests were needed on either of us.

I had discreetly explained to Warren that I wanted all the tests done on both of us. I did not want John to feel he was being singled out, especially as I was much older. It would be of comfort for us both.

He said he would do a cognitive function test with John while Sharon, his nurse, would do one with me. We undertook the tests separately; I think I got it all right.

On entering Warren's room, John looked at me sadly. "Robbie, I don't think I did so well. What about you?"

Warren quickly reassured us. "We must analyse all the results, so don't jump to conclusions, okay? Just because you think you got something wrong doesn't mean a bad result."

After an anxious week, we arrived to see Warren for the results. We waited nervously until we were called in. After the pleasantries, Warren spoke.

"I will get straight to the point. Johnno, you have signs of early onset dementia. However, it is early, and we can put in place procedures and medication to help manage it. I know this will be hard to take in and you will both have questions. I will make an appointment for you both to see a neurologist who can give us a more detailed report. He may call in others if he feels there is more to explore. Your physical fitness and a stable relationship are a great plus for you both.

"Are you fine with that Johnno?"

He nodded yes, then added, "Did any football injuries bring it on?"

"Nothing of any significance showed up. However, age can affect everyone differently. Robbie basically has good health, but there are some issues with his heart which we will need to monitor."

"Is it serious Warren?"

"No, Robbie, but it does need to be monitored. We'll do annual check-ups and ECGs."

Taking his hand, "John, this is just another hurdle for us both; we know how to deal with those."

Warren shook our hands, and patted Johnno on the back saying, "Go well guys," as we left.

When we got to the car, I said, "John, you drive."

He hesitated.

"It's early. We go on as we always have, or I will crack the whip."

Amiably mumbling, "Bloody novelist," he slid into the driver's seat. "Let's get a coffee, okay?"

I nodded as we took off. He drove to the local drive-in, got coffees, and headed off. I soon realised we were heading to our park, the same one where we had coffee after Jimmy's party. It had become a special place for us.

We sat down and I put my arms around him as his head sank into me, sobbing. After a while, I heard him chuckle.

"What's so funny, young man?"

He looked up at me smiling, "When I got together with you, some people asked why an 'old man'. You will be lonely when he dies before you. Sadly, it now looks like the other way around."

"Not necessarily. You heard what Warren said, we both have issues, and it is early days, so we think and work positively at it, okay?"

"I can never argue with you, old man." I kissed him and we held each other for ages.

"I know it's not Friday, but can we have pizza tonight?" and together we shouted out, "No anchovies!" My smile said it all.

We arranged a visit to the boys to tell them about the doctor's visit. They were all thrilled to see us as usual, and our grandchildren made a fuss of Grandpa and Bo-pa. Lisa made tea, and we all sat down. John and I decided we needed to get to the point straight away.

"Your dad and I saw our doctor a couple of days ago for a check-up."

"Spit it out Robbie."

"Well, lately we have noticed your dad has been having some issues with his memory, getting a little confused and becoming a bit agitated in the evenings. To cut a long story short, we know you will both know all about early onset dementia." Everyone nodded solemnly.

"They gave us lots of information to read. I only hope I don't get all the things they say. I could never be violent to Robbie, or some of the other things."

Huy was his usual empathetic self. "Wow, that's something for us all to digest; we are all here for you."

"The doctor has said it is early days, so we need to adapt to what is ahead of us."

"We will look after you," added Liam, wiping his eyes.

"Thanks guys. Robbie and I must get on with our life. We need to learn how to adapt. We're grateful we've had so many years together; this is just another curve ball. We've had a few of those in our lives!"

"Dad, Bo, you can stay here as long as you like," offered Huy.

"We know that, but your dad and I need to be in familiar surroundings to adjust. You are still close enough for lots of visits in the future. Time will tell how our future will unfold. One of our plans is to visit Ubud again. Let's say a second honeymoon."

"Oh," said Huy, "too much information." Laughter from the boys and Lisa. We could always rely on them to make us feel loved.

After that visit with the children, John and I sat down and decided we needed to plan the future routine around the issues we would face. After discussions, we asked Todd and Adrian over for drinks. John was tearful when telling them, apologising for not wanting to catch up with them because of his health. They were sympathetic, hugging us and saying they were there for us.

Todd had been surprised when John suddenly said he was considering transferring the business to him. Todd had told John he would only take it over if he bought it at a fair market price, but John refused.

John had become very agitated, which had alarmed Todd. Knowing John so well, he knew something was wrong. He and Adrian even discussed coming to see me. However, Todd felt that would be going behind Johnno's back; he had too much love and admiration for Johnno, so they didn't contact me. After much discussion, they agreed a pension would be paid to John each week in lieu of a purchase price.

Todd was pleased we had told them, and it was out in the open. They reminded us that they would be there for us in any way they could.

We told them we had decided to base ourselves at Alex Headland, sell the Brisbane house, and replace it with a unit for city visits. John wanted a house at Alex Headland. However, I pointed out the courtyard was big enough for John's orchids and plants. As a bonus, we could easily lock it up to travel to the boys and go on holidays. If need be, we could commute by train to Brisbane, but we both felt that was a long way off. John looked at me, saddened, knowing what lay ahead.

Trying to be helpful, Todd proposed, "We could always drive you anywhere."

John reacted badly, shouting, "No, we can manage!"

"Thanks guys,' I murmured to diffuse the situation. "We know you are there for us. John and I will continue on as we always have." John weakly smiled.

Later that night in bed John snuggled up, "I know they all mean well, but together we will soldier on, old man."

"Indeed, we will, young man," as we drifted into sleep.

CHAPTER 46

Sometimes, you wonder if it is wise to do a last visit to a special place you hold dear in your heart. It could be a sad visit, knowing it is the last. However, we decided to do it and make it just another Bali trip.

Ketut, as usual, collected us and took us to Ubud, through the throngs of traffic, to the villa we liked to call our own—our second home. Agus, our room boy, greeted us with such affection. He knew our routine, and we slipped into it so well.

John's condition had changed our routine somewhat, but we adapted to that; being together was all that mattered. Every moment now was precious.

Each day we walked; we knew the place so well. It was a comfort to us to be in such familiar surroundings, and it made it easier for John. We always had coffee at Café Luna and lunches at our favourite restaurants. Fortunately, few people recognised us now. Some days were better than others, but like so many couples, we worked through it. These times were tough, but we had been through tougher. It always seemed easier together.

Our nights together were still our time, although age and health had caught up with us. Our kisses, cuddles, and intimacy in bed were still our very special moments, although now they had lost the intensity of when we first met. But the magic was still there.

John was always urging me to continue writing, so I did. He loved sitting with me as I typed because I constantly gave him things to research for me. We had always worked well together, and this was a special time for us. I wanted to keep his mind active. I refused to allow any thoughts to creep in on what it would be like without him.

❍

When we returned, Huy and Liem came down for a weekend to share time with us at Alex Headland. Sadly, John's health had deteriorated more quickly than expected.

The boy's visits, although short, became more frequent. We were concerned that it put pressure on them, but they were insistent. They knew visits by us to them were difficult.

We loved our walks at the beach, and coffee at the Alex Surf Club kiosk. We had many good times there together over the years, but now we knew time was limited, so every moment counted.

Each week, we eagerly waited for news from Millurat. John wanted every detail, loving the photos and videos they shared. We did not dwell on the fact that we would not visit the town again as a couple.

On what was to be one of their last visits, the boys suggested a late afternoon drink on the headland overlooking the beach. We had picnicked there so many times over the years. They produced bubbles and glasses, and together we toasted a wonderful life. We talked about the wonderful times we had enjoyed together, with the boys expressing how their lives were enriched by us. We treasured our two sons enormously.

When John took my hand, I reflected on how many times he had held it. What a rich journey we had shared, from when I first saw that smile at Jimmy's party. Drinking in the sunset, we four held hands and remembered. John smiled at me, the fading light making his eyes glisten brightly. We four were together.

As the weeks went on, John continued to deteriorate and, with the help of carers, I managed to ensure John had some quality of life. I did what I could, and the carers always made me feel as if I was the one shouldering the burden.

My writing had come to a standstill. Not only had I no time, but I had also lost my drive for it. When our doctor said time was short, Huy and Liem came down to support us both in John's final days.

❍

I remember the last day as I lay with John on the bed; the boys curled up around us. We chattered away about all sorts of funny things that had happened to us; all the highlights we had together. John joined in when he could with short bursts.

It was a long day until he finally looked at me and mouthed, "Love you." His eyes closed, and silently, he slipped away. The three of us lay there not speaking for ages. You could not describe the silence in the room.

The boys took my hands, and we walked out of the room, knowing they did not want me to feel the warmth of his body leave him.

We sat outside in the garden as the sun set. My boys, either side of me, held me as we sobbed. I never slept in that room again.

EPILOGUE

Bo died soon after Dad. Bo had never told any of us how ill he was; he always wanted to be there for his John.

It left a gigantic void in our lives. Our dads had been there for us for so long. They had enriched our lives, giving so much of themselves for us, but still allowing us to retain our heritage. We were two young boys truly blessed.

In accordance with their wishes, they were privately cremated, their ashes mixed and scattered at Alexandra Headland, a place of happiness for them both.

We share, dear readers, with you, something special.

We found a large box marked Our Story. Bo had kept incredible records of their life together. In reading it, we, their sons, wanted to share their journey with you. The journey of two men who proved that you can rise above anything and find true love.

Liem and Huy

www.ingramcontent.com/pod-product-compliance
Lightning Source LLC
Chambersburg PA
CBHW030411310726
48979CB00002B/372
* 9 7 8 1 9 2 3 2 8 9 9 2 5 *